D1197256

"Lindsay Hunter won't be caught lie-telling in the name of nice. The miniature stories in Daddy's are fierce and unapologetic. When the We's she voices say the axblade was bloody with dirt, what they mean is the neighbor's swingset creaked and moaned next door and we heard a child's voice say Never ever. When I'm looking again for my next undoing, I'll crack open Daddy's, and get the true news they tell us we'd be better off not hearing."

   –**Kyle Minor**, author of *In the Devil's Territory*

Daddy's

24 fictions by

Lindsay Hunter

featherproof BOOKS

Published by
***featherproof* books**
Chicago, Illinois
featherproof.com

First Edition

10 9 8 7 6 5 4 3 2

Library of Congress
Control Number: 2009944042

ISBN 13: 978-0-9825808-0-6
eBook: 978-0-9825808-8-2

Design: bleachedwhale.com
Set in Serif Beta by Betatype

Printed in the
United States of America

for the city of ocoee, fl, from the years 1986 to 1996

with love to my family and ben

TABLE OF CONTENTS

MY BROTHER

My brother tells me monsters set up shop in his closet among his Reeboks and hidden *Playboys*. Yeah, he says, leaning back and stroking his chin, yeah, you can't see it but something's coming for me. Big whoop, I tell him. We drag his record player out and aim the needle at the middle of "Rocket Man." He makes something up. He says, I got two sisters and they're both girls. He says, I'm bored to death with all these nightmares. He says, I'm pretty sure Dad's a pussy.

My brother went to jail a couple times. My sister and I told people, God don't take revenge. We said, We accuse the world of pretending at the sky. To each other we said, Our brother is in jail. We pressed numbers into phones and hoped for an answer. I got one once and it was, Your brother is a baby giant stupid in a cage. My sister got one and it was, There's a light around your brother and it's an ugly shade; pray for something.

My brother called collect and then sat around. He said, You know what I been thinking? I been thinking a lot about *Jeopardy!* and driveways and sex. He said, I been having sex with the wrong people. He said, Remember how the driveway tilted up and the house looked like a red idiot at the top. He said, I'll take amnesia for four hundred, Alex.

My brother held the phone up to his ear and pretended it was a horn. My dad watched him on the TV screen. My brother said, Wilma? and my dad got irritated. My brother tried to put on a good show. Dad, he said, I just don't know what's wrong with me. Behind him a row of tubas blasted a note and he gestured at them. He said, I got this kind of chorus behind me. He said, They never shut up. He said, I can't stay on too long I got some soap to drop. He said, I need a drink of something too strong and my dad nodded like a man hanged.

My brother digs a hole and buries most of my dad in it. He says, If we talk nice to it it'll sprout roses. The record player plays our favorite song. It says, That's whiskey in your veins and blood on the moon. It says, There'll never be another night like this. My brother hands me the shovel and says, King me.

SCALES

My brother is a fish, I tell Yesenia.

We're sitting by her pool. Yesenia is wearing a black bikini and when she stretches I can see her pubic hair. I'm wearing jeans and a sweater. Her weight barely makes a dent in the pool chair; I'm so heavy that if I move slightly I can feel the concrete deck under my ass. We're tanning under the gray sky, smoking the last of the pot we found in her sister's sock drawer. Every few minutes I think I hear thunder, or a garbage truck.

Yeah, she says. Wait, a *fish*? Then, holding her breath, she says, You're high.

Right now, I hate her. The way she smokes like she's not really smoking, like she's just mimicking something she saw in a movie, squinting her eyes and laughing like she would if she was dying of laughter—*huc huc huc huc*. But I press on.

It's not like he has gills or anything, I tell her. But he's been staring a lot, and sometimes when he's really deep in thought his mouth opens and closes, like he's gasping for air, and his feet are really flat and wide, like flippers.

You mind if I cash this? she asks, holding up the joint, and then cashes it. You love your brother, she says.

I want to tell her something that would shock her—something like, I had a dream I was licking your dad's hairy chest, or, The lightning in your eyes looks like cinnamon floss, or, You're ugly. Something to make her listen. Something to make her see me differently. But I just say, Yeah, I love him.

Let's go inside, she says. I'm freezing. My nipples are like little rocks—*huc, huc, huc*. Plus, she says, winding a towel around her dry hair, we can weigh ourselves on my mom's new scale. It's digital.

My heart sinks. I'd rather not, I tell her. I had a breakfast burrito and I don't think it's digested yet.

Whatever, she says, walking away, her bottoms creeping into her asscrack. Then she wheels on me. You think I care? she hisses. Her hip is cocked; her towel is so tight it makes her eyes turn up. She doesn't elaborate.

No, I tell her. I don't think that at all.

I follow her in. Thunder. Definitely thunder.

In her mother's bathroom, Yesenia stands naked on the scale, her bikini crumpled in the sink. I make a point of looking anywhere but at the scale. I concentrate on a picture of Yesenia's mom and stepdad standing in a combed white desert, smiling and sunburned.

I hear her dismount the scale, then mount it again. *Godfuckingdammit*, she whispers. I stare so hard at the picture that their heads come alive, floating out from the frame, circling each other. They get so close I notice what looks like a peppercorn in Yesenia's stepdad's teeth.

Get on the scale, Yesenia says. She's standing in front of me, arms crossed over her belly. I can't get her into focus—I can still see her parents' heads floating around, zooming in and moving away, until they finally settle onto her breasts. And then I realize I'm staring at her breasts.

Get on the fucking scale, she says. Her face is red and wet, tears streaming freely.

Yeah, okay, I tell her. I get on the scale and she crouches to read the numbers. Her spine sticks out and in the bright light of the bathroom little shadows collect under the bones.

Ha, she says, standing. I still weigh more than a hundred pounds less than you. She takes her bikini top out of the sink and wipes her face with it. Let's go find something to eat.

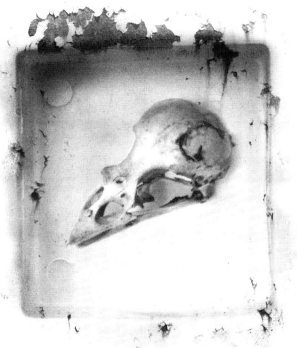

In the kitchen she piles a tub of ice cream, spray cheese, Doritos, a six-pack of Diet Coke, and pretzels onto a tray. We put it between us on the couch and she sits, cross-legged and naked, and watches me eat. Is that good? she asks. That looks really good.

I eat slowly. Every once in a while applause soars from the television and I mentally bow. I don't even know why the television is on—she watches me, and I watch the food.

I eat until I can't eat anymore. I'm done, I tell her.

Okay, she says. Good. She puts the tray on the floor and scoots closer. I give her my hand and she sucks my fingers clean. The thunder is so loud it drowns out the television, but I watch it anyway—a talk show, a woman openly sobbing, a child stunned by the lights, the host stabbing the microphone into the audience. Who has something to say? *Say* something, say *something*. Yesenia's mouth is warm, and even though I can't say I like it, it's soothing, and it feels good.

When she's done she flings my hand into my lap. I try not to be obvious about wiping it on my jeans.

This is a dumb show, she says.

I know, I tell her.

She leans in and kisses me, licking my lips, probing my mouth for bits of food, sucking my tongue. I keep my eyes open, watching the fading dots of her parents' heads dancing around the room.

She finishes, leaning back into the arm of the sofa, rubbing her arms. I'm still cold, she says.

So get dressed, I tell her.

You're not a dyke, are you? she asks.

I shake my head. No.

She nods to herself. Good, she says. You should go— my stepdad's going to be home soon.

At the door she says, See you tomorrow.

I leave my bike at her house and walk home. The thunder is so loud it sounds like hunks of sky are crashing all around me. I make it to my street before it starts raining thick drops that sting my skin. I'm drenched by the time I can see my brother at the window, staring out at this sea of rain, his mouth closing, his mouth opening, his mouth closing. I lie on my back in the yard and let the rain fill my mouth. I wonder how long I can stay like this before he thinks I'm drowning. Probably forever.

THE FENCE

My husband, Tim, came home on his lunch hour and we had sex on the floor next to the oven. I could see our reflection in the black glass door and when Tim turned his face toward it I saw his flared nostrils, his neck thick with effort, and I turned my head so that I was looking at the island in the middle of the kitchen instead. Near the end I saw an ant scuttling through a tiny hole at the baseboard. It went toward the living room and I remembered the coffee I'd left on the coffee table, and wondered if it could smell the coffee from here, and if it would drown in pursuit of the sugar I'd stirred in, but I was still able to come. Concerned, our black Labrador, Marky, came over and started licking at the beads of sweat on my face. I pushed him away and he trotted around the island to sniff between my legs, his wet nose flitting at the inside of my thigh. When I clamped my legs together his head got caught, and he yelped.

"Hey, hey, hey," Tim cooed, still on his knees. He scooted over to Marky and scratched his ears and under his collar. "Want me to rub your belly? Let me rub that belly, there we go." Marky lay on his back, his paws jerking with pleasure.

Tim took his sandwich to go and called me from the car. I could hear him chewing. He said, "I'm still hard. I liked that. Love you." When we hung up I gave Marky a bacon treat.

After I cleaned myself up I went to the fence and then I went again just before Tim came home—he thought I was out there to greet him, and I let him believe it.

I woke up to Tim's hand on my arm, trying to roll me over. "Hey," he whispered, "come here." When I turned to him I could see over his shoulder that it was 5:13 in the morning. His breath was hot in my face and he didn't bother pulling my underwear all the way down—just enough so that he could maneuver. He guided me onto my back and then he lay on his side and I folded my legs over his, my underwear stretching from knee to knee. He held me by the hip and pushed himself in. He was done quickly, and he fell asleep with his head on my shoulder. Marky never stirred from his place at the foot of the bed, though he did begin to dream, his legs jerking and his mouth quivering, a low whine coming through his nostrils.

When Tim left for work, his hair still wet from our shower, his fingers playing with my zipper, I turned Animal Planet on for Marky, removed his collar, and went to the fence. It runs the entire length and width of our property, but I have my favorite corner, right where the gravel driveway stops and the grass starts, where I can see the road and if I stretch I can touch our mailbox. The fence is invisible, but it's there. I wind the vinyl part of Marky's collar around my hand, holding the plastic receiver in my palm, and then I press the cold metal stimulator against my underwear, step forward, and the jolt is delivered. Like a million ants biting. Like teeth. Like the G-spot exists. Like a tiny knife, a precise pinch. Like fireworks. I can't help it—I cry out; my underwear is flooded with perfect warmth. I lie back in the grass and see stars.

I try and think of my husband when I go to the fence, but he becomes a distraction, and sometimes when I conjure him up I can't go through with it, and my trip is ruined.

Tim barely made it through the door. He pushed me up against the doorjamb, tugging at my zipper. His was already open; I could see his bouncing penis through the glass panes at the door as he walked from the garage.

My pants fell around my ankles. We were in an awkward position—my legs couldn't open enough—so he spun me around and bent me over the table that he threw his keys on each night when he came home from work. Its top was intricately tiled in the shape of a large green turtle, its legs splayed and its eyes weirdly on top of its head. My front tooth caught some of the grout during one of Tim's thrusts, and when I cried out he said, "Yeah. There we go. Like it, don't you." Still, I came, shuddering until my knees buckled, nearly rocking the table onto its side, and then Tim came, heaving at my back in long dry sobs. Marky lazily watched us from his place on the couch, his eyes slowly shutting and then bursting open at every new sound.

"God, I'm starving," Tim said, his mouth hot and wet at my neck. "Do we have any M&M's? Peanut?"

He left soon after that, a red Dixie cup full of M&M's in one hand while the other swatted at his crotch. "Sore. In a good way. You too, I hope," and his eyes were so full of genuine interest that I pushed him out the door, bowing my legs in answer. He mimed stepping over the invisible fence, looking back to see if I was laughing, and I wondered if my trips out there were the cause of the sudden urgency of our sex life, if he could sense something was different, if the fence worked on him even without him knowing about it.

I watched his car back down the driveway, then I waited for the cloud of dust it kicked up to settle, and then Animal Planet, collar, jolt, wet explosion and sleep.

The phone was ringing when I came back inside. I put Marky's collar on and let him out, and then I answered it.

"I just saw you lying in a heap in the grass. I told Fred to stop but he said he could see you breathing even though we were going thirty-five miles an hour and that you were probably just sunning yourself. I told him if we see on the news that our neighbor was found dead in her yard and we didn't stop I'd never forgive him for as long as I live. So you're fine, you're alive?"

"I was just playing with Marky. Playing dead." Cradling the phone at my shoulder, I peeled off my pants and underwear. I could see the bruise under my pubic hair—a sunburst of purple and blue. It was tender and sent a zing of pain through my groin when I touched it.

"I didn't even see Marky. Well. You want me to come over? You want to have tea?"

"Some other time," I told her. The brightness of the bruise wasn't helping—I'd been trying to work up the courage to hold the collar to my bare skin.

"Kiss that husband of yours for me. Bye bye."

Outside, Marky was running from edge to edge, his body bucking. Twice, he got too close and his body froze and he screamed like his heart was broken, like he was being pulled apart.

Over spaghetti, Tim pulled me onto his lap and rubbed himself against me and finished without even unzipping. He held me there, rocking me and kissing my chest and neck tenderly. I unzipped him and wiped him down with a napkin, wetting a corner with my tongue.

We watched television, his body cupping mine, his fingers in and out of my underwear, idly exploring. Marky was on the other couch, scratching his neck with his back paw.

"Fred called me today," Tim said. "He said the sounds Marky makes when he runs into that fence are god-awful. He could hear him this afternoon all the way down by their place."

"He's just getting used to it," I said.

"I don't know," he said. "Look at him." Marky was rubbing his neck on the arm of the couch. He'd scratched and rubbed the collar until it was up by his ears. "I think we should get rid of it. Marky doesn't need it anymore. He knows where he lives."

I reached into my pants and took Tim's hand and brought it up to my mouth, taking in the two fingers that had been inside me.

"Oh my God," Tim said, and grew hard. I guided him in from behind and in the middle of it all my arm landed on the remote and the TV turned off and then flickered on and Marky watched and I wondered if he was waiting to see if it would be Animal Planet.

Tim fell asleep with his legs entwined in mine and it took me many minutes to disentangle, but I finally did, making my way in the adjusted dark, closing the door silently behind me. I made sure to remove Marky's collar before we went to bed, and it was on the turtle table where I'd left it, coiled awkwardly. The alarm we never seemed to turn on gave its three warning beeps—a door is opening—but it was loudest downstairs, and I knew Tim wouldn't hear a thing.

The grass felt good under my feet, I couldn't tell if it was wet or cold, or both. It was like walking on one of those massage pads at those gadget stores—a welcome, dull pain. At my corner I reached under my nightgown and pulled my underwear down and held the collar to the skin just above where my pubic hair stopped. I told myself I should be afraid, that this could really hurt, but then I leaned into that invisible boundary, and it was wonderful. For a moment I was convinced I could feel it in my fillings. I moved the collar down and leaned in, the feeling was so intense that a few drops of urine escaped and clung to my thighs.

On my back in the grass the night sky looked close enough to touch and then I had the strange feeling that I was floating, that I wasn't lying in the grass, that I was rushing up too quickly into the night and that I would break through the layers of the earth to freefall through space forever. It was the loneliest feeling and I left my place in the grass and went back to the house and up the stairs to our bed. The room smelled like sleep–like deep breaths and sheets and the warm bitter musk of bodies–and when I lay down Tim turned over in sleep and molded his body to mine and Marky let out a long sigh. My underwear was wet and cold and I wished I had taken it off.

Just before lunch a man in a white hat and overalls came to disable the fence.

"Your husband called me?" he said.

The damp strap of Marky's collar dangled from my finger behind my back; I'd run into the house from the fence when I'd seen the man's truck pulling off the road onto our driveway. Beneath my skirt, my underwear was around my knees and I was sure the man could smell the sharpness of the urine.

"I'm here to turn off your fence?" He said it like, "ye fayuhnts?"

It was over in fifteen minutes. The man walked to the four corners of our property and aimed a large square remote at them and punched at the keypad, then came inside and took Marky's collar to be recycled. When he was outside I'd pressed a wet cloth to it. "I washed it. That's why it's a little wet," I told him.

Before he left he told me that the fence was disabled, but that if we ever wanted it turned back on to call him, that it was still there. "Everything's as it was," he said. "The only thing missing is the electricity. The spark," he said, patting Marky's head, "for Sparky here."

Tim came home and when I was bending to take his potpie from the oven he pulled the sweatpants and underwear I'd changed into down to my knees and stuck his pinky in my anus. "Okay?" he whispered into my hair. I held onto the stove and watched myself in its flat surface, Tim's face appearing suddenly, his eyes closed, mouth open, a lock of hair loose on his forehead. "Oh. Kay. Ohh. Kay," he said.

He ate the potpie with his fingers, sucking them triumphantly when he was done, even, at one point, the pinky that had been in my ass.

At the door he kissed me, the flick of his tongue at my bottom lip. "God, I love you. I really do. I'm positively joyful," he said, "giddy."

I watched him back down the driveway, his hand in a flat wave. I let Marky lick the potpie dish, let him push it across the floor until it bumped against the baseboard. When I took the plate away Marky went to his water bowl and drank, his big tongue making sloppy, satisfying sounds. When he was done I let him out, collarless and free.

I filled the sink with soap and hot water—as hot as it would go—and plunked the potpie dish into the suds. From the window above the sink I watched Marky bounding from edge to edge. He believed the fence was still there and stopped just short of its boundaries, stopping to pee, shoulders hunched into it, a powerful yellow stream. Then he sauntered over to the edge and didn't stop. He stepped through the fence and onto the driveway. My hands were red and swollen in the water, my fingers picking at a blob of crust on the dish, and Marky continued on down the driveway and turned right at the road and disappeared into the woods at the far corner of our property.

I put his water dish in the suds and cleaned that, too, and then I went upstairs and lay on our bed and wept until my ribs were sore. I went into our bathroom and straddled the edge of the tub, and it felt good to have something hard and cold there, but not nearly good enough.

UNPREPARING

My boyfriend and I have sex and when we're finished he holds me close and whispers into my ear, I just date-raped you. What do you do now?

In the grocery store he throws an avocado at my head from 200 feet away. I duck at the last minute and he yells, That could have been a grenade.

It was an avocado, I tell him. Yes, he says, yes, but what if it wasn't?

He asks me to stop at the drugstore on the way home from work and when I'm rounding the corner near our apartment he jumps out of the darkness in a ski mask, brandishing one of our Ginsu knives. Your purse, he hisses, hand it over. A woman comes up behind me and makes a noise, a startled Oh! and then runs the other way, her shoes slapping the pavement. Honey, I say, lifting up the mask. He's snarling, baring his teeth, and I pull the mask back down.

My mother says, It's a phase. All men go through phases, she says. Phases always end.

One day the little boy who lives above us finds my boyfriend at the bottom of the stairs with blood all over him. The paramedics come and haul my boyfriend to the hospital and on the way they discover the blood is fake—maybe colored corn syrup, though it smells like ketchup in places. The little boy had just learned 911 in his kindergarten class. I get a call from the hospital to come pick my boyfriend up.

He's waiting for me in the lobby. I wanted you to find me, he says, his voice cracking. I wanted to see what you would do if someone murdered me. His face crumples.

I know, I tell him, putting my hand on his back, leading him to the door. One of the paramedics approaches us on our way out and says, Yo that was fucked up, what you did. Seriously. He has a wide smear of my boyfriend's fake blood on his forearm. I pull my boyfriend out the sliding doors before he can try and explain himself.

The next morning I wake up to his hand on my shoulder. He says, Do you think I could fight off an alligator? What about a shark? Or a lion?

No, I tell him. That'd be the end of it for sure.

This makes him mad. I hear him in the shower, raking the soap across the tiles, lathering it up so that when I get in I'll slip and fall. I decide not to shower, rolling on extra deodorant and putting my hair into a ponytail.

That evening he picks me up from work. The radio is on so loud that the seat underneath me is throbbing. Over it he yells, The unexpected is everywhere. Danger is our only real home. I just want you to be prepared. Then he accelerates, offroads it, drives us into a tree. I feel my ankle and wrist snap, almost at the exact same time. My neck starts to stiffen. When I look at my boyfriend he's grinning at me, blood pouring from his mouth. My face hit the steering wheel, he says. I think I broke my nose. A sprain at the very least. I've never seen him so happy, so alive.

The paramedic from before picks us up. He swipes a finger at the blood on my boyfriend's chin and tastes it. Just wanted to be sure this asshole wasn't faking again. I love you, my boyfriend tells him. I really think we could be friends. The paramedic is enraged, spluttering, Fuck off. Kiss this. Shut the hell up.

At the hospital a cop with an ink stain on his shirt asks me if I want to file charges. I say Maybe? Later a nurse comes in and wakes me up, leaning so close I can smell the hazelnut coffee on her breath. You're preggy preg pregs, she says, rubbing my arm. Did you know that? About eight weeks along. I wonder if it was the time my boyfriend pretended he was an HIV-positive man going around and infecting people or the time he pretended he was Jack the Ripper and I was a good-hearted prostitute.

I tell my boyfriend the news and his eyes light up. What if, he says, what if someone kidnapped the baby? For ransom, or to sell it on the black market? What if you tripped and fell and landed on your stomach?

I don't know, I tell him. He turns on the news, says, Come on, get to the terrorist stuff.

When he leaves to get coffee I imagine him spilling the coffee on himself, getting third-degree burns that fuse his fingers together. I imagine him getting stuck in the elevator, the cables breaking and the elevator plummeting him to his death, though the hospital is only three floors high. I wonder if it's possible that an air bubble got injected into his bloodstream in the crash somehow, that it will reach his heart and he'll go down, his heart exploding like a firecracker in an apple.

After a few minutes he comes back, watching the coffee in his cup, trying not to spill. The colors on his face have deepened, purple around the eyes fading out into green and yellow. A bit of blood in his nostrils, black and dried. I am so disappointed to see him unharmed that I start crying. The tears come hot and fast; I cry so hard my neck sings with pain. Hey, hey, he says, coming over and taking my hand. Hey there, I know. I know how you feel. It was fucking awesome, right? Dropping my hand, he reaches over me for the remote.

The nurse comes back in, tightens my sheets, checks the IV bag, says cheerfully, Yep, still alive.

THAT BABY

The baby was normal when it came out. Daddy snipped the cord like nothing, the baby screaming silently till the nurse sucked out whatever bloodsnot was stuck in his throat, then there was no turning back, it was there, his voice, his mouth wide and wider, that baby was all mouth, his cries like a nail being driven into rotten wood. Normal.

Daddy said, Let's name him Levis, we always liked Vs in names, and I'd heard the name Levis before but couldn't place it, and besides, that baby was a Levis, it was obvious.

We took Levis home and he sucked me dry within an hour. Daddy went to the store for some formula and Levis ate that up too. I made a pot of mashed potatoes for me and Daddy and the baby did his best to stick his face into it, his neck nothing more than a taffy pull, his big head hanging so I could see the three curls he'd already grown at the base of his neck, sweaty, looking for all the world like pubes lathered with baby oil, and I shuddered looking at them and chalked that feeling up to postpartum.

Levis wouldn't let Daddy sleep in bed with us, he was clever that way, soon as Daddy slid under the bedcovers Levis would start screaming, that nail torturing that rotted wood, that endless nail, then when Daddy would get up for a glass of something the baby would quiet down, and Daddy and I aren't stupid so soon we figured Daddy could get familiar with the couch for a while if it ensured Levis acted peaceful, and I gave Daddy permission to tend to himself in that way as much as he needed to since I was busy with Levis and couldn't do my wifelies.

Levis grew at night and plenty of mornings I'd wake up to see him lying there with his diaper busted open. Other ladies I've known who have given birth had always chittered on about their babies' growth spurts, but here Levis was 40 pounds within a week and 60 midway through the next, hair on his knuckles and three block teeth scattered amongst his jaws, then when he was one month old he called me Honey, his first word, fisted my breast, his nails leaving little half-moons in my flesh when I pried his hand from me, his grinning mouth showing a fourth tooth, a molar like a wad of gum wedged way back.

Daddy and I had heard of ugly babies, of unnaturally big babies. We'd seen a show once where what looked like a 12-year-old boy was in a giant diaper his mother had fashioned out of her front-room curtain, sitting there with his legs straight out in front of him like he was pleased to meet them, his eyes pushed into his face like dull buttons, and the mother claiming he wasn't yet a year. But Levis wasn't on the TV, he was right there, his eyes following Daddy across the room, those eyes like gray milk ringed with spiders' legs, and at two months Levis had chewed through a wooden bar in his crib, splinters in his gums, him crying while I plucked them with a tweezer, me feeling that nail in my gut, me feeling something less than love.

We took the baby to the doctor, Daddy explaining that there was something off about Levis, he was big, he didn't look like other babies, he had teeth like a man, and Levis quiet and studying Daddy like he understood, twirling his finger in his nostril, around and around, pulling it out tipped with blood. The doctor weighed Levis and he was up to 75 pounds and his third month still a week away, the doctor asking what on earth we were feeding him, warning us babies his age shouldn't be eating table food, and me and Daddy scared to say that the night before Levis had lunged for a pork chop, screamed until we let him suck on the bone, Levis making slurping noises like he was a normal baby, like the bone was his momma's nipple, his cheeks like two halves of a blush apple. The doctor sent us home, told us to watch what Levis ate, get him a jumpy chair for exercise. The doctor reaching out to pat Levis' head, then thinking different when Levis grabbed his wrist, the doctor blanching at the thick hair on Levis' arms, Levis giggling like a normal baby playing, just playing.

During bath time that night Levis' baby penis stiffened and poked out of the water, Levis saying HoneyHoneyHoneyHoney in his husky baby voice. I called Daddy to finish the bath so I could lie down but Levis screamed until I came for him, wrapped him in a towel, him freeing an arm to reach up and stroke my cheek for all the world like I was his, like he had me, and there was that stiffy again when I was fitting him with his diaper.

At six months Levis walked into the kitchen at breakfast and tried to open the fridge himself, Daddy stunned and dropping scrambled eggs from his mouth, and Levis speaking his next word, Pickles. Pickles, Honey, he said, pounding on the fridge door with his hairy chunk fists, and I sliced some bread and butter pickles up for him and that's what he had for breakfast, a whole jar, me noticing that he was only a foot shorter than the fridge door, could almost reach the freezer where Daddy kept his vodka.

One night Daddy turned to me and we began our special time, I let Daddy do what he would since it had been so long, but soon enough I noticed Levis standing in the doorway watching, that finger in that nostril, and when I made Daddy stop Levis climbed into bed between us and began tp try feeding, something he hadn't done in months, falling asleep with my breast in his mouth, like any other sweet baby, I told myself, like any other sweet baby boy, Daddy going back to his couch for the night, his shoulders hanging heavy, like the pillow he carried was a stone.

At eight months Levis opened a drawer and found a paring knife, held it to Daddy's gut and giggled, a sheen of drool on his chin, finally pulling the knife away when he got distracted by the ladybugs printed on his T-shirt. Then Daddy left, saying Levis wasn't right, saying he needed to get away, saying he'd be back, driving away while Levis watched him from the window, his baby man hands flat to the window, like everything he saw could be touched that way, me watching Daddy's headlights cut the dark and then the dark crowding right back in behind them, Levis saying Honey? to whatever he saw out that window, maybe even to himself.

Levis came to bed with me, molding his body to mine, rubbing his face on Daddy's pillow sleepily, his breath like garlic, like garlic and meat, didn't even open my eyes when he reached for my breast in the early hours and fed himself. In the morning he woke me, whispering Honey, Honey, smearing the sheets in elaborate patterns with fingerfuls of poop from his diaper, twining his fingers in my hair, Honey.

Normal. Later I bathed Levis and dressed him and we went to the park. For a while I pushed him on the swings, waited for him at the bottom of the slide, did the seesaw with him. When Levis was playing in the sandbox another mother came and sat beside me on the bench, said Your boy is quite large, me saying Yes, me saying Thank you. The woman's son got into the sandbox with Levis and they started building something and the woman went on, said I'm a producer for the local news and we'd love to have your boy on if you're interested, as kind of a feature on local unnaturals, and Levis looking up and showing his teeth, his eyes slitted at the woman, like he heard her, like he understood.

Maybe, I told the woman, when Levis is a little older, the woman saying Fine, fine, smoothing her jeans like she was peeved at the color of the wash, and her son getting up to bring his fat little shoe down on Levis' sandpile, over and over, saying Unh Unh Unh, Levis letting him for a while before grinding a fist of sand into the boy's face, the boy just blinking for a minute like his second hand had stopped, Levis taking the opportunity to grab the boy by his ankle and bring him down to where he could pound on his abdomen with his fists, like any baby with a toy drum, like any baby figuring out how hard to pound to get just the right sound, the boy going Unh Unh Unh.

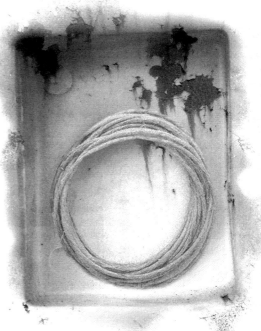

The woman said, My Lord, do something, he's flattened my Jared, her running over like her legs were breaking out of concrete molds, her boy saying Unh a little quieter now and me more proud of Levis than I'd ever been and so getting up and walking to the car, Levis saying Honey? Levis standing up to see better, saying Honey, stepping over the boy and out of the sandbox, me getting into the car and locking the doors, key in the ignition, Levis just standing there, the late afternoon sunlight giving him a glow, just standing there with his fists at his sides, looking like a fat little man more than anybody's baby, a little fat man beating his chest now, me pulling out onto the road, Levis wailing Honey, wailing Pickles, getting smaller and smaller in the rearview until I took a turn and he was gone, my heart like a fist to a door and my breasts empty and my nipples like lit matchheads.

IT ALL GO BY

We almost hit a deer on the way up but we swerved just in time. The sky was a hundred million dilated pupils. Then on the way back down we saw a deer dead on the side of the road with its legs up like it was laying on its back and stretching up its legs in order to admire them better.

It ain't the same one, you said.

I put it out of my mind and watched the lines on the highway. Lines, even though as fast as we were going they looked like one long line, anyone knows it's a bunch of lines running together. Eyes playing tricks. If that's true maybe we did hit that deer and just put it out of our minds and let our eyes go abracadabra on us. Either way.

One thing about night is that it can always get darker on you. There we were in the middle of a country highway, not a car around, and the darkness started getting to us, creeping in under our collars the way a stiff wind sometimes can. I remembered all those times Mother talked about someone walking over her grave, the chill bumps on her arm that stayed for nearly half an hour. You said, We're almost there and when I looked over you were dark outlined in dark, dark things rushing by outside your window that were probably just trees in the median.

Pretty soon you pulled off the highway and headed west for a bit. Then you pulled into the parking lot of a pancake house. We're here, you said. I said, Are we? You laughed to yourself, said, Les' go inside, get somethin to eat.

We crossed the parking lot toward the door. The car was settling behind us, a bunch of sighs and clicks. It was thirty-two steps exactly to the door, a shame, since I guessed twenty-seven.

You picked the table in the corner by the window, fogged the window with your breath and traced a big X into it. You said, X definitely marks the spot.

The waitress came over, recognized you, said, What can I get ya in a voice flat as a country highway. Oh, you said, I believe I'll have a cup of Sanka and a piece of cherry pie. My counterpart here will have an iced tea and a grilled cheese. The waitress walked off, her shoes squeaking, or maybe it was just one shoe.

You said, You know, I'll bet someone aimed for that deer.

The only other customer in the restaurant got up, stomping his feet like his legs had been asleep. He paid his ticket, said, Y'all have a good night now on his way out the door. I watched his taillights until they were as small as the deer's eyes were in our headlights, until they were gone.

It's just human nature, you said, to want to kill. Pure instinct.

Our food came, the waitress dropping your plate in front of you in a clatter, the coffee sloshing around in your cup but settling before going over the side. The tea was cold and sweet and reminded me of antifreeze and I drank it down in three long sips. I pushed my grilled cheese over to you. You dug the cheese out with your forefinger and spread it onto your pie.

You know what, you said, I feel a lot calmer with you here in front of me. I tried to remember where I'd heard that before but the closest I got was one night when I was twelve or thirteen and I snuck out to go swim in the swimming hole. Some friends were supposed to meet me but never showed, and I forced myself to jump in anyway since I went to all that trouble. My foot touched something slimy and I shot up quick, and did the backstroke for a while, and then I just tried to float for as long as I could. The stars that dotted the sky were as white as little baby teeth and twinkled like diamonds, and it was a queer feeling—and this is the closest I came to remembering where I'd heard what you said before—it was the queerest feeling, what with my front nearly bursting at all that glitter and joy and my back tense and frightened of what swam underneath.

I excused myself and went to the bathroom, locked myself in a stall. I sat on the toilet seat for a while, just enjoying the quiet, then retaped the knife at my ankle. I had a delicate little cut where its edge got too close but nothing to holler home about. I let myself out and stood in front of the mirror, watched myself draw the gun from inside my shirt and aim. My face looked greenish and strange under the bathroom lights. It only had one bullet in it, but of course I didn't tell you that.

I was about ready to come back out when the waitress walked in fluffing at her bangs. I pretended to wash my hands while she pulled lipstick from her apron and smeared it on, took the pins out of her hair and put them back in, blow her nose. On my way out I saw that she had a runner in her stocking right behind the knee.

You were eating a second piece of pie, bits of cherry sticking to the corners of your mouth like blood under a neon light. My glass was full again, the ice shifting as it melted, a little puddle of sweat in a ring around the base.

Yep, you said, scraping the plate with the side of your fork, no getting around it. We're animals, and we have instincts.

I drank my tea down. You went and paid the ticket, the cash register ding hanging in the air for a good few seconds. I thought of my single bullet, thought of shooting a hole in the night sky, making some kind of light.

The waitress took my glass, squeaked into the kitchen. I wiped off your X with a napkin, pushed my face into the window and watched it all go by: our car in the parking lot where we'd left it. Those thirty-two steps. The highway, making that rushing sound even when there weren't any cars on it. All that relative dark, all them dark trees. That deer admiring its legs for all eternity. Us. Me. That swimming hole and that swath of stars. How I'd shoot the bullet directly above the deer so the light would shine right down upon it, how I wasn't sure why. And you, standing there with your hand inside your shirt, looking like something that was just on the tip of my tongue.

FOOD LUCK

You remember that time we entered that contest and I ate 37 pies and you got to 38 and launched a barf-wave over the crowd. You remember how then as a joke I got down on my hands and knees and ate it up, even made slurpy slurp slurp noises as I went for the maximum joke effect. You remember how Mom made me walk home but you remember how I still got that ribbon, boy. I still got that ribbon. Still got it. Blue with gold lettering and a couple flecks of your barf.

What about that time we entered that hot dog–eating contest and you choked on number 16 and I took my folding chair to your back. A chunk the size of a cocktail wiener shot out your mouth and into the crowd and I'm not sure what happened to it after that, if I knew at the time I'd have gone to get it, you best believe that. By that time Mom was too fat to drive so I drove us home and you bitched the whole way that your back hurt and it hurt to sit back against the car seat and you needed some ice and maybe a doctor, but you got over it. Later I'm saying. Later you got over it. You remember how you wouldn't let me into your room that night, how I slept on the floor outside your door and then we went down for oatmeal in the morning just like always.

You remember how we went on that double date and I dared you so hard to drink four large milkshakes in a row because I could do it no problem and you got red in the face when Deandra turned and asked Why, why couldn't you do the same thing. Deandra ate two burgers and a large fry herself that night, and later on I drove her and her friend home, her friend who was supposed to be with me, but me and Deandra parked in the empty lot behind her house and did it after we dropped her friend off, and Deandra smelled like grease and onions and talcum powder, and remember how you weren't there to put a stop to it because we left you in the bathroom of the restaurant. Remember how that was the right thing to do because you didn't want the girls to know how you got the runs down both legs, how you left your jeans in a wad behind the toilet and walked home with your jacket tied around your waist. And all the while Deandra saying Mmm, mmm, all the while me and Deandra feasting in the backseat of Mom's car.

Remember how Mom would eat a dozen eggs and a pan of bacon, and remember how that one Christmas she went to stretch and found an old brown napkin wedged in her neckfat, how then we wanted to know what else was hiding in there, a diary, a housekey, a slice of pizza, and hey remember when we joked that Dad was in there somewhere, because that was how we dealt with Dad leaving us and moving in with the man who ran the movie theater. We made jokes about it. Like how remember that one time I made you laugh when we drove by Dad cutting the man's grass and I yelled Hey faggot out the window as we passed. At least I think you laughed. Didn't you? Or like that time we tried to see how many different things we could fit into our mouths, marshmallows, grapes, hunks of sandwich bread, and I said Hey this must be what Dad feels like when he's got that movie theater man's testicles in his mouth.

What about that time when I came home with six gallons of milk from my job at the Circle K and told you I'd believe you were a man if you could drink one whole gallon per hour, and I even unscrewed the tops for you so you wouldn't have to stress about that, and you made it three quarters of the way through the first gallon before you bent over the kitchen sink and rolphed it all back up, and I said you should just go ahead and move in with Dad, and Mom heard and made a sad walrus sound from the other room and I told her to shut it and said it was time for you to drink the next gallon, but you refused. You with that chunky yellow dribble on your chin, looking up at me from your crouch over the sink, saying, No sir, No sir, over and over again. And me not telling you that I'd tried to get to one gallon an hour and failed, that somewhere on the drive between the Circle K and our house there was a pretty little puddle of just-turned milk that I'd blorted from the car window, and that I'd only gotten through the second gallon, nowhere near six.

And then there was that day we had a dinner for you because you were leaving and I had the lady in town make you a five-layer fudge cake with a crushed potato chip layer, and on the top in script she wrote Food Luck instead of Good Luck, and I didn't say anything when I picked it up because Food Luck was goddamn right, you know? And how Dad came over and didn't bring his friend and Mom took a washrag to her neck and upper arms beforehand to freshen up and put a flower in her hair from the bowl of potpourri on her nightstand, even though she couldn't leave her bed to greet Dad at the door, and then when he finally showed she called out, So lovely to see you Fred, and Dad said And you, Tee, but they never actually saw each other. And then I told Dad you'd eat the entire cake, crumbs and all, and how proud he'd be when he saw it, but Dad left in a rush after you threw up in your mouth and then swallowed it back down just like I'd shown you, and I yelled Good riddance, Gaywad, which I know he heard before he shut the door behind him, and I told you to stop crying and finish your cake, and you did, and then the next day you left and got your college degree and a wife and a little son you named after Dad.

And Mom dead a year and buried in two plots to accommodate her size. And Dad living in the city with a different man now. And me here all this while so hungry, eating pies, eating cakes, eating bags of pretzels hot dogs sugar crystals chocolate bars pizza wheels gallons of milk pints of liquor a million beers marshmallow fluff peanut butter loaves your old teddy bear the drapes in the living room Deandra's panties a collection of river rocks fistfuls of mud an old tire a rusted padlock a ring of keys a baby tooth an entire pumpkin the nails from my fingers the hair from my head any blood I emit and all those bits of the highway that get kicked up every time someone drives out of this town.

WOLF RIVER

Johnson communicated he could go for a lunch. In the corner office our boss had his head in his hands. An orange balloon floated by the window. Johnson whispered, More than anything I'd like a beer, an apple turnover, and some pussy. Right about now. The orange balloon hovered, caught on something. Our boss said, Goddamn it all Jesus Mother of God and the balloon freed itself. Or the wind freed it. It went up and I watched it reflected in the glass building across the way. Tiny bit of orange.

I'd once gone camping with a girl. She built a fire the way her grandpa had shown her. Or maybe it was an uncle. Teepee of kindling. Match. Puckered lips blowing until the fire could breathe on its own. We burned the weenies and then the marshmallows. Shared an apple instead. The girl told me about this river in her hometown, how its banks were rocky and gray. How the rocks looked like wolf bodies. How she pretended it was a river of wolves. As the fire was dying she howled into it. Like this, she said. Swim in. I put my hands on her, then in her. The fire spit and crackled. A last ditch. The girl quit howling.

Our boss waved a twenty in the air. Coffee black, he said. Johnson wondered which diner had the least slobby waitresses. The orange balloon was a black dot, a floating period in the sky. Johnson said, Tits. You know? I tried to remember what happened to the girl. Europe maybe. Or some kind of nanny position somewhere else. But anyway, that orange balloon and that orange fire. Stamping out the urge to howl in the elevator. Then me and Johnson hitting the sidewalk, a different kind of river.

THIS ONE

You wake up. Put just a T-shirt on because those jeans eat at your ass and it's too early for that yet. You make what your daddy proudly called hillbilly coffee. That guy in your bed is moaning in his sleep, pointing his toes. His junk's all shriveled and caught up in that black tangle. You think how if that were you you'd be more modest, even in your sleep. You think, I don't believe I like this one very much. Then you remember putting your mouth on that thing, just for a second the night before, and how grateful he seemed, how his body instantly went from tense and strong to flop-relaxed and jelly, how that alarmed and disgusted you so you pretended it was just a stop on the way to kissing his lower abdomen. Now you rub your tongue against the roof of your mouth to equalize the bitter taste, a taste close to the one that time your mama boiled the hot dogs in the pot of de-limer your daddy was using, you sick for days after only a couple bites. It was a accident, you tell people. You'd probably say that now, should there be the same people in your house staring with you at this man with the thick rope chain around his neck and the missing molar. It was a accident. I needed a ride. You laugh to yourself, Lord did you ever need a ride.

And now the man is waking up, doing snow angels in your bed and yawning wide. You think, I should not allow him to see me standing in the doorway watching him. You think, that would give him some kind of wrong idea. But after he is done fisting the sleep from his eyes he sees you anyway. You think, let him. The man smiles, and maybe it's not a missing molar, maybe it's closer to the front than that. His hands are at his chest, scratching his nipple area. Girly, he says to you, I got me some morning wood. You see for yourself but it ain't promising, looking like it's on the other side of wilting. A lazy type of erection. You remember your daddy warning you about lazy men, saying Check the hands darlin, the uglier the better, your daddy missing the nails on both thumbs and always offering your mama his index finger to use as a nail file. You don't remember the feel of this man's hands. You couldn't pull his hands from a police lineup. You say to the man, nodding toward that mess of a crotch: That ain't much to write home about, but it is more like you've said it to the room and the room has soaked up your quiet tones and anyway the man is yawning again, doing that thing people do when they feel right at home, stretching and yawning something closer to a shout than a yawn.

There's coffee, you say to the man in a louder voice. You want to get the ball rolling. You imagine yourself enjoying a quiet morning once the man has left, staying in your T-shirt until the late afternoon, and then who knows. Maybe dinner in front of the TV. Maybe a stop by the bar. It all seems like years in the future. You are pleased at the thought. The man starts playing with himself. The man is left-handed and this fact seems to render the man special somehow. You think the words Handicapped, Disabled, Special. No one in your family is left-handed. You realize that maybe you've only ever encountered left-handed people on the TV. Don't drink coffee, the man says. I drink something else, and there's that hole in the gums again, he has apparently said something suggestive to you but you're having trouble picturing exactly what he means. You realize if he closed his mouth and his eyes you'd probably give him another go, due to that left-handedness. And maybe you've said that last thing out loud because his eyes snap shut and he purses his lips, his tongue roving around, but maybe that's just his usual masturbating face. That hand gets faster, the flesh at his belly shuddering.

You are having a hard time with this man's comfort level in a stranger's house. It seems rude to you to feel so at home in a place that isn't his home. But despite yourself you are turned on. You feel disgusted but inflamed. You tell yourself it's that left hand. It's downright exotic. In you go, your ankles cracking at the first few steps. You straddle the man, yank the crotch of your underwear over because getting them off would take forever and you barely have seconds before the magic of the moment would subside. The man pumps three times before pushing you off. Your underwear snaps to. The man says Hoo-eee. He wipes himself off on your top sheet but misses the dollop just under his chin.

You and the man lay there. You study the swollen corner of your ceiling, decide to pop it with a safety pin sometime soon. You wonder if that would be a big enough hole. The man gets up and in the blurry corner of your eye he is dressing himself. He goes into the kitchen and you hear him touching things in your refridge. He reappears in your doorway and you watch him unpeel a slice of cheese from its plastic sleeve, then mash it into a cube. You wonder if he is trying to fashion a new tooth. You got damn near fuckall to eat, young lady, the man says. Your daddy used to call you young lady when you were in trouble. You think, Am I in trouble? The man walks over and kisses the air over your hairline, holding his crotch like it aches. The man says Damn, says your name, which you don't remember telling him. When he is gone you think about getting dressed, calling someone, going into town. You think about doing a lot of things. Instead you lie in bed and listen to a neighbor down the road mowing his grass, the sound of that motor goddamn ripping you to shreds.

OUT THERE

People burn cars out there. My father took us out there when I was eleven and we burned GranGran's car, him shaking the lighter fluid over the hood and up against the sides like he was seasoning it, then he let me and Lily toss the lighter through the passenger window but we had to promise to run as soon as it left our hands. 'Less want me to roll you in hot sauce and eat you like a crispy wing, you'll run your little asses fast as you can. We kept our promise and felt the fire at our backs but didn't get to see it start, when we turned around it was going like it'd been alive forever.

Later Lily asked me did I see the fire reflected in Pop's glasses, did I see how it looked like millions of goldfish swimming up the lenses. You were watching the wrong fire, I told her. I beg to differ, she said. She'd heard this somewhere and had figured out a way to use it, I could tell by the smug way of her mouth and how she was exhaling through her nostrils.

Another thing to know about out there is there's a pack of wild dogs that claim it as their home. The story is that a farmer loaded up his sheepdog and her puppies one day, drove out there and pushed them out of the truck because he couldn't bear to drown them but he couldn't afford to feed them either. People hear that story and get disgusted but some of these same people have driven the family dog out there and set it free to join the pack, Pop did that to Jinx but said it was good news, Jinx was with her own, was back roaming the desert sands the way God intended, and all I could think was how Jinx didn't have that many teeth, who would soak her food in water so she could get it down? I've never seen the dogs but if you're out there burning a car or anything else at night you can hear them barking in that wounded way, a whole choir of them sounding like they're being kicked or shot with BB's.

The point is Pop knew both of these things. A place where people come to burn cars, a place where abandoned dogs eat sand or each other: these are not comforting facts. But that did not matter to Pop. What mattered was tradition, albeit a tradition starting with me and Lily. This is your legacy, he shouted at us from inside the car. Your rite of passage. If you make it you will be men. If you don't I'll lickety-split a prayer for each of you come Sunday. Then he peeled out, left us coughing in his dust. Lily said, Don't he know we're girls? How are we supposed to become men then?

It didn't take long for Lily to start crying. Some book she read described how an orange sun is the deadliest, how letting its rays coat your skin is akin to taking a lye shower, how the orange was from God's bloody iris, when I asked her if that meant the sun was God's eye and if so was he a Cyclops she slapped her own face, said she had itches under her skin, it was the orange rays coming for her. She took off running. I let her. In the flat desert I knew I could see her for miles.

Then I learned a third thing about out there. I was watching Lily run, her arms up to shield her, looking like a shimmering exaltation not a hundred feet in front of me. I looked down at something itching my calf and when I looked up Lily was gone. Wasn't even a dustcloud in her wake. That's the third thing. The desert is a warp master. Lily warped or I warped but either way the desert opened up its coatflap to take something in and when the coatflap closed again I was alone. I knew it wasn't any use but you have to go through the motions when something shocking happens. I called Lily's name. I spun around in place. I followed her footsteps but they petered out and I wondered if I was back where I started. I screamed for her till the sun came down, then I sat in the sand and watched the unlikely colors in the sky, the purple and the silver and the green and the white white line of the horizon which was the last to go.

The dark out there was a navy quilt sewn with pearl buttons. There was part of a moon wedged in the sky that gave off a dull glow. The dogs started around then, yelping and whining and getting closer and closer. I brought my knees up to my chest and concentrated on my shoes because I could see them, they were a fact, they were indisputable, I remembered putting them on in the morning, I remembered retying the laces after school, how they were black in their creases from when I jumped into the lake wearing them months before. A furry thing knocked against my back, knocked again, it was terrible in its boniness, it rubbed against me like a cat, a tongue swiped my arm, paws clawed at my legs, they were crying like they were trying to hold it in but couldn't. They smelled like mothballs and corn chips and old blood.

Pop always talked about mirages, how they happen outside of the desert all the time, like television, like the produce aisle, like any woman in a wet swimming suit. What I noticed first was the black flickering, I wondered how I could see black flicker in all that dark, then my eyes saw the rest of it, saw the orange flames which formed the black flicker, saw them shooting up, undulating tall, saw the fire, saw the fire, saw the fire, and I ran to it.

The desert is a good lesson in life. It proves that what you want most will most likely stay out of reach. That fire was mine, was my love, was the breath in my lungsacks. I heard the dogs behind me singing their brutal chorus, I knew they remembered what it was to beg, that fire moving fast toward the end of the earth.

But out there is different from your typical desert. Because it was Pop burning up our car, drinking from a milk jug, Lily sleeping in the sand like a punished doll, and by the time I reached them the dogs were gone, weren't making a peep. That Jinx you were running from, Pop asked, laughing wide. His glasses got the worst of the black flicker and I decided not to look at him directly, possibly forevermore. When Lily woke up we thumbed it home.

FINDING THERE

He drove. Called his best friend from a motel with a swimming pool. I don't know if I can go on.

Everybody thinks that, his best friend said.

He had a wife and some kids. With every state line they became more like lace drapes in a window, with every state line he had to remind himself to miss them. He didn't know how hard it could get.

In New Mexico the clouds had stretched across the sky like blown sugar. In Oklahoma he poured a jug of water into his engine. He pretended his car was a great paintbrush, that he was leaving a black creek behind him.

He watched the news, the free movie, the scrambled-porn-channel oil painting, turned the volume up to hear the uh, to hear the oh, to hear the yeah, you like it.

The nights were fine. They were dark, they were the bottom of something. At twilight he pressed his stomach into the railing outside his room, swallowed what he was missing into the watered-down sky.

At a Golden Griddle in Alabama he met a woman at the counter. Bought her a cup of coffee and watched her stir it one way and then the other. She pressed her finger into some spilled sugar, told him she was missing the part of her tongue that recognized sweet. At that, his eyes filled.

Back in his room she stood at the foot of the bed and undressed. Her thighs were toned, bits of pubic hair peeked out the sides of her underwear. She bent, crawled up the bed, straddled him. The air conditioning kicked on, light came through the windows lazily, he thought of his middle daughter holding something up, saying Can you open it? He fucked the woman, those were the words he used when confessing to his best friend days later. He didn't tell his friend about the scar he found over her heart, a scar that had teeth, didn't tell his friend that she asked for money and he gave her everything in his wallet, that he'd asked to braid her long black hair and she'd laughed at him and walked out and left the door wide open, him on the bed naked and sweating and empty every which way there was to be.

He kept driving. Veered toward the Gulf and rented a room a block from the beach. Kept his shoes on as he waded into the water for fear of jellyfish. It felt natural to be pulled by the tide, to be tempted to let it take him, and then for the tide to finally let go and push the other way. He stood like that for some time, dipping in his fingertips at one point and tasting the salt. He saw a shark's fin on the horizon and it wasn't until later that he realized it was probably just a sailboat.

On the way back to his room a teenaged boy said Hey man, you got any change? and then, You want a date? He brought the boy back to his room, sat on the bed and waited while the boy went into the bathroom, locked the door, turned on the water. He put the TV on, some kind of soap opera, interrupted by a weather report hinting at a tropical storm in the next day or so. The bathroom door opened and the boy walked out, wet hair, no shirt, drips of water running down his neck, hands shaking. His heart filled and he stood up, put his hands on the boy's shoulders to try and calm him. Don't worry, he started to say, and the boy punched him in the sternum. It wasn't a hard punch, but he guessed that it was supposed to be enough to knock him down, so he played along, landing on his stomach, clutching at his chest, moaning, trying for breath. He reached into his pocket and pulled out a twenty, held it in the air like a small green flag. The boy took it, backed away from him, called him a pervert and then a motherfucker and then a perverted motherfucker, opened the door so hard that it slammed into the wall. He could hear the boy's boots on the metal steps outside, then as they ran across the parking lot. Only then did he push himself up onto his knees, wipe the carpet bits from his face. The weather report was showing an animation of

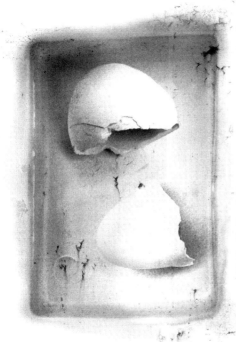

the tropical storm growing until it covered half the state. The weatherman assured him that it wasn't a definite, but that he had to be prepared.

He sat on the bed for a while, watching families walk by his open door with towels and snorkels and baggies of sandwiches and cookies, looking in at him and then looking quickly away. He walked to the 7-Eleven on the corner, bought a pint of rocky road and a couple MoonPies. On the way back to the motel the sun was an orange yolk sliding down the sky. He forced himself to look into it, but after a short time had to look away.

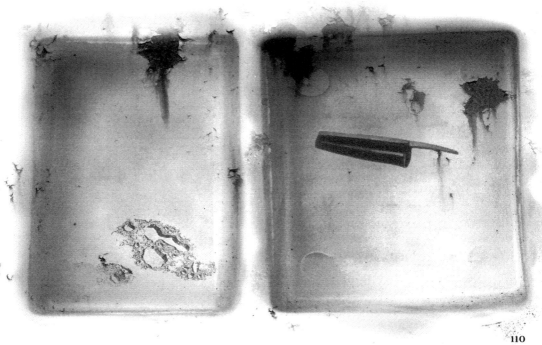

Back in his room he thought for a second about hanging himself from the shower rod. Ate both the MoonPies and started on the ice cream, turned on the evening news. Someone had been abducted, a small girl with saucer eyes and messy hair. In the morning he'd drive north, make another state, maybe two. He finished the ice cream in four large spoonfuls. It slid down his throat and iced his heart. He pulled the covers up to his belly, wondered what he could leave of himself behind and all he could do without, thought of how his wife often had lipstick on her teeth, how it made her look like she'd just bitten into something alive, something that bled. At a commercial break he picked up the phone, dialed home, hung up when he heard his daughter's voice, small and distant, singing Hello, Hello, Are you there?

NOTE

I wrote my sister this note about all the things I hate. Gorgons, it said. And how people go nutville any time the moon throws a shape. Nasty ass Nilla Wafers. The smell of crotch, which only seems to come wafting out from my sister's room. Football players and especially football players who spend time in my sister's crotch-smelling bedroom. The way the cable box gets all warm so Daddy knows when he puts his hand on it I been watching my shows instead of doing my papers. Cats, but not kittens. Arm hair. Cutting the grass on Sundays 'cause Daddy didn't have no sons. Thigh chafe. Sun-In. Hair that has Sun-In in it. Hair from my sister's head and finding clumps of it in the drain or in a tangle breezing around the bathroom floor. Anything orange-flavored. I hate, I said, and then I corrected myself by crossing out hate and writing despise above it, but not crossing it out so much that she couldn't still see the word hate, I despise shit in other people's teeth. Namely peppercorns and chewed-up bread products. But then I got specific and said Shit like them threads, them *filaments*, I said, that get left behind and flutter from between your teeth once you bite into a orange slice and have swallowed down all the juice and loose pulp, because my sister sure did like a good orange slice. The words loose and pulp coming anywhere near each other, come to think of it, I said. And also, the smell coming from the kitchen drain. That spoon that got caught up in the kitchen drain that I keep getting stuck with which is surely mangling up my lips with every bite of store-brand breakfast whatever. Lip chap. People that don't brush the mung off they tongue. The sound of two tongues meeting somewhere in the middle, like slurp-slap, slap-slurp. Any song by that one guy. Any song that could be described as a song to get kissing to. Any boy that makes any kind of noise loud enough for me to hear as I happen by my sister's room on my way to none of your business. Any boy says Jesus like anyone else'd say Mark or Dave. Thick lines of dirt in some fingernails. How cologne smells like toothpaste and rubbing alcohol. How Daddy walks around shirtless. How I can't help but notice the swirls of hair around Daddy's nipples. How Daddy has nipples in general. The word nipples or any word starting with the letters N-I-P. How Momma farts when she's doing her exercises and no one reacts. The VHS that's been sitting on top of the TV since last summer labeled For Adults Only. Adults in general, and how they seem unaware of things like fate and magic and daughters who are losers and music that is current and candy that ain't Hershey's. How God is I guess an adult too.

How attractive Jesus is in his pictures. And anyway, I said in this letter, I hate how Momma buys store-brand feminine products with names that always end in O. TampOs. MaxOs. And then also how you answer everything with Oh. It's 8:30, where're your school books? Oh. That boy you shut in your bedroom the other day was manhandling a girl that wasn't you over behind the library. Oh. Your face is a shiny clock without no hands. Oh. And alright, I hate the following things about myself: big boat feet, mosquito-bite chest hints, plague of freckles, can't sing, brain feels swole all the time, but least I don't go around offering up my tater on a platter for a cocktail party of wieners to lay up against, and least the cat ain't got my tongue when I see you in the halls, and least I can look at a jar of buttons and see it for what it is whereas you look right at something and see all them dances to come and boys to kiss and stars to count while you laying in the driveway looking up and I'm laying in bed looking nowhere.

PEGGY'S BROTHER

We play truth or dare and it keeps getting worse. I run down the driveway and back up again with a hot dog in my teeth and my bikini bottoms in a wedge, I am on all fours, my naked butt in the air, a turd-like swirl of toothpaste on the small of my back, my best friend Jessica licking it off and gagging, I am dared to eat one of the twins' boogers. This I don't do. I take one look at it, dark red in the center, both dry and glistening, and I run to the bathroom and lock myself in.

Peggy's mom's soaps are shaped like seahorses; the one in the bathtub dish has been worn down into a featureless grubworm. I hold it in my hand, its underside slick and cold, while the other girls knock on the door, say, Come on you don't have to eat it, and Shelley wiped it on Peggy's brother's door so don't worry, and, from Jessica, You're being boh-ring.

After I hear them walk away and pad down the hallway, I come out. Peggy's brother's door is open slightly, I can hear the low tones coming from his television. The last time I was over at Peggy's he'd woken me up and I'd had to step over the other girls as he led me into his room and then he just held my hand, rubbing my knuckles with his thumb so hard that the next day my knuckles were red and chapped and my mother rubbed Eucerin on them for a week. That was all. He'd held my hand and then he'd dropped it and opened his door, waited for me to leave, and then closed it behind me. In the morning we ate cereal across from each other and he told Peggy he'd farted into her box of Corn Pops.

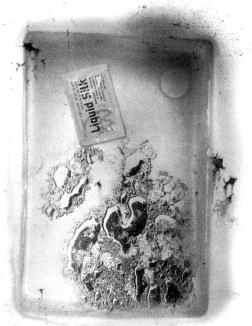

I hear Grace say, I am seriously going to vomit, which means the game is still going on. I knock on Peggy's brother's door and then, when I hear one of the girls coming down the hallway, I duck in and shut the door gently behind me. Peggy's brother is watching *The Shining*, waves of blood rushing down a hallway, two dead girls laying askew. I'd watched it many times at Peggy's house, and it had always seemed funny, too dramatic, we roared with laughter at the little girls asking Danny to Come play with us, forever. But here, in Peggy's brother's room, it is suddenly terrifying, Danny's face frozen in fear, the stifling browns and gold of the hotel, Danny's mother's crowded, gnashing teeth.

Hey, Peggy's brother says. Come over here.

My face is hot, I feel goldfish in my stomach and I trip on a basketball making my way over to him in the dark room. He laughs quietly. There's nowhere else to stand but in front of him, stretched out on the bed, his feet crossed at the ankles and sheathed in white gym socks.

Sorry, I say, for blocking your view.

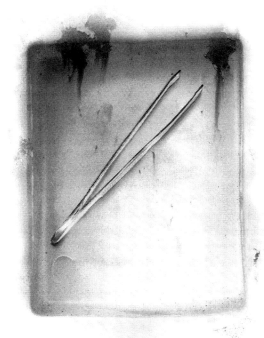

It's no biggie, he says. He takes my hand again, pulls me onto the bed next to him, and we lie like that, side by side, looking up at his ceiling, at the flickering pattern the leaves make on his ceiling, at the flickering blue light between each leaf.

Have you heard of fucking? he asks, raising his voice over Danny's mother's screams.

I think so, I tell him.

Good, he says.

Oh, definitely, I say.

After a few minutes he reaches down, pulls my nightgown up. I'm going to look at you, he says. I hear the toilet flush, try to keep my voice as quiet as possible when I say, Okay.

He doesn't pull my underwear down like I thought he might. Instead he uses two fingers to yank the crotch over to the side, and I have to open my legs a bit wider. I can feel the breath from his nostrils down there, he is taking deep, calm breaths. It smells a little, he says. Not a bad smell, but definitely a smell. An odor, really. But again, not bad.

Oh, good, I say. That's good.

Hang on, he says, and jumps off the bed, pushes things around on his desk. Danny's father brandishes an axe, smiling, laughing. When Peggy's brother comes back he has a magnifying glass and a flashlight, and when he is next to me again he pulls the panties over with one hand, holds the magnifying glass in the other, bites the flashlight between his teeth. He prods a little, the way my mother does to her pizza dough on Friday nights, then pulls the two folds apart.

Wow, he says, the flashlight bobbing up and down. It's so ugly, but in a very great way. You know? I want to look at it forever.

The flickering pattern on the ceiling flickers faster, the wind picking up and faintly whistling, and I remember my dad telling me at breakfast that it would rain tonight, folding one corner of his paper down to look at me, then snapping it back up once I'd said, Oh, really? Oh yes, he'd said, we are going to have quite a storm.

It's this thought, the thought of my dad in his work clothes in our yellow kitchen this morning, reading the paper, letting the dog lick bacon grease from his fingers, that makes me want, more than ever, to get out of Peggy's brother's room. I have to go, I tell him.

Wait, he says, holding me by the hips, spitting the flashlight over the side of the bed and tossing the magnifying glass over with it. He locks eyes with mine, and I feel dared, I recognize the dare whirling behind his eyes, feel his heartbeat pick up against my thigh, and then he is lowering his head, I see the heart-shaped bit of his scalp at the top of his head, I feel his soft lips, hear the same smacking kiss my mother used to place on my forehead at night, hear him say, I just really wanted to kiss it. And then he lets my underwear go, lets the crotch snap back in place, he pulls down my nightgown, says Don't step on my magnifying glass on your way out.

When I leave, Danny's father is limping through a snowy maze.

In the living room the girls say Where the h-e-double-hockey-sticks were you? and You missed it—Grace and Peggy just touched each other's boobs for fifteen whole seconds, and It's your turn—Truth or Dare?

Dare, I say, and I'm dared to go outside in the rain and roll naked in Peggy's mother's garden. Which of course I do, because the garden is right underneath his window, and maybe somehow that makes me part of what comes through his window, part of what's flickering on his ceiling, part of those shapes, part of that light, part of that blue blue light.

LOVE SONG

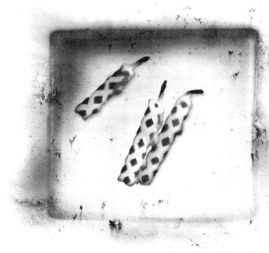

It was my birthday and Daddy picked me up and he was drunk and we drove to the mall and I waited at a Ruby Tuesday's and ate me a pot of French onion soup while Daddy did the rounds at the various jewelry stores trying to sell jewelry from God knows where. I sat by a window so I could see him at the Kay's across the way and he was showing the turquoise rings he wears on his own hands to the lady behind the counter and it was clear she was ready for him to move on. She had on a red turtleneck that made her boobums look all cone-shaped and I wondered did she stuff her shirt with some kind of funnels? She folded her arms up under them things and it just made the situation all the worse, and then Daddy leaned over and poked the lady right over her heart, he was making some kind of point that appalled the lady with its passion, passion's a big thing with Daddy, and the lady dropped her arms and looked around her and out into the mall hoping someone would come in for a watch or a pair of earrings and save her, and then Daddy leaned back, holding his palms up to show how harmless he was, then pulled his pinky ring off and shoved it onto the lady's finger. Daddy calls that going in for the kill. The lady held her hand out like he'd taken each finger into his mouth and sucked off the salt, and Daddy flicked one of his business cards onto the counter and backed out, holding his palms up again, like, Look at me everyone, I just tamed a wild beast and made it my wife. After a couple steps he tripped on the carpeting and the spell was broken, his hands flopped down to his sides and he looked around like he'd been beamed there from somewhere else, and he turned on his heel and went around the corner and disappeared, on his way to the Zales or the Jared's down at the other end of the mall. The lady with the pointed boobs shook her hand till the ring fell off and I couldn't tell where it landed. She reached down and brought up a spritzer of blue cleaning solution and spritzed her hand a dozen times, then wiped it with a cloth. Her hair was askew and I knew she was rattled, but she'd get over it, everyone gets over it, or they don't.

I drank me four more Cokes and then Daddy come back in with his tie all undid and one of his shirttails hanging out looking like it had recently been wadded and then dipped in something wet. He slid into the booth and took a swallow from my fifth Coke, said You need you some kick to that, girl, brought out the flask from his coat pocket and poured in a fistful of something colorless, took a long pull, muttered, Good girl through wet lips. He played with a dinner roll, the rings on his fingers clinking quietly. She was a twatter, ain't she? he asked, gesturing with his forehead toward the Kay's. The roll looked all punched through and hollowed out and Daddy put it in his mouth and stood up, tucking in his shirttail. Let's hit it, he said.

In the car Daddy had on the music real loud, singing "I ain't never been with a woman long enough / for my boots to get old / we been together so long now / they both need resoled. / If I ever settled down, you'd be my kind / and it's a good time for me to head on down the line." He turned it down long enough to say, You listen real good girlie, they's lots of truth in this song. He had both windows down and his tie was blowing every which way, the wind playing in his hair, his smile showing gummy bits from the roll, and I could tell he wanted me to glean something real deep from the song, something about him, but sometimes hard as you try meaningful moments like that are just moments like any other, the sky up in the sky and traffic going by and Daddy stopping playing the air flute just long enough to swerve around a semi and his breath like something aflame. "Always something greener / on the other side of that hill / I was born a wrangler and a rounder / and I guess I always will. / Heard it in a love song / heard it in a love song / heard it in a love song / can't be wrong."

We turned into Gator's, Daddy's favorite establishment, and as we parked he belched my name, drawing it out, something I used to love, then he added I planned something real special for you on your special day, his breath going out at the last word, sounding wet, him pounding his chest a little till the red in his face turned to pink. Shew, he said in his normal voice, then Damn blast it! when he dinged the car in the next spot with his door as he got out. I need me a drink, he announced, hoisting up his pants, breaking into a jog toward Gator's.

Inside, the music was loud and Daddy did a little soft shoe up to the hostess. Darlin, we have a reserve, he said, under Birthday Girlie. The girl walked us over to a small table with two stools. These your menus, she said, but we out of chicken fingers because they spoilt the other day. Daddy ordered a double whiskey and two Cokes, and when the hostess wandered off he presented me with a Ziploc of quarters. Happy Birthday, sweetness, he said. That's enough for at least two games of eight-ball, if you can stand it. You ready to get your tail whupped? The flatscreen on the wall behind him was playing the Home Shopping Network. A woman with a helmet of hair gritted a smile and held a doll toward the camera like it was radioactive. The word BEAUTIFUL was stamped across the screen in urgent block letters, flashing like a neon sign on its way to burning out.

Daddy racked and hit all the solids into the pocket, pointing at me and laughing with every ball sunk, but he got distracted by his third double whiskey and seemed content just wilting into his stool while I watched a man swab what looked like streaks of blood off a woodgrain floor with a supersize Q-tip on the TV. A lady walked by and Daddy's eyes lit up and he lurched off the stool and grabbed her elbow. The woman's hair looked fragile with bleach, her face pocked and her eyes lined in blue. She smiled at Daddy and I could see where she was missing one of her bottom teeth. Honey, he screamed, this my girlfriend Sewanee. The lady threw back her head and laughed like her throat was working metal against metal. Is that what we calling it now, she said when her head was righted. Daddy laughed and said, Yeah and it was obvious he hadn't heard what she said. This my child, he told the lady. She's sixteen today. Pleased to meet you, the lady said, holding out her hand like I should kiss the leathery knuckles. She leaned in, said Let me ask you, you a tough bitch yet? You made of chain mail yet? I could smell her cinnamon chewing gum and her powdery perfume. When I didn't answer she said You work on that. Work on getting mean, hear? Daddy was swaying and staring hard just to the right and

I knew he was trying to get back his focus. I put my hand in his, said I got to go home now and do my homework. The lady patted Daddy on the cheek and sat herself at the bar and Daddy slurped down the rest of his drink and followed me out the door.

It was dark out, the lights in the parking lot doing more to make the sky look dark than anything, and Daddy fumbled for his keys for a while before they spilled from his pocket and landed at his feet. I'm fixin to drive, I told Daddy. Aw-ight, Daddy said, but don't be thinking I ain't still got a pair, girlie, your Daddy's just all fucked up tonight and empty as a pocket.

On the highway Daddy drifted off, his snores like a clogged chainsaw. I held my breath in the dark spots between streetlights. Daddy woke when I took the exit ramp, twitching hard and rubbing his nose. You notice how things that's ugly look pretty when it's nighttime? He pointed at a gas station as we passed. Like look how gorgeous that is, that white light through them windows and that solitary Indian clerk just existing inside. It probably smells like donuts and hot dongs in there and I'd like to go in and talk with him, Daddy said. I wish I could talk to everyone on this earth. Suddenly he put his hand up on his mouth and held it there a minute, and when he took it away he whispered You cain't hold your liquor down, you don't deserve to drank it.

I pulled up to Daddy's apartment. The lights were off and I wondered did that make it ugly to him. Here we are, Daddy, I said, and Daddy snorted, said Here ain't it, girlie. We there, we not here. This is there. You get me? I helped him to the door, him putting all his weight on me and smelling good, like aftershave, and bad, like something pickled in sweat and rubbing alcohol. When we got inside Daddy lurched head first and landed on the couch, rasped Happy Day of Birth girlie, you suck a gopher's asshole at pool and just 'cause you sixteen don't mean you can get to going around with any boys. I flipped the lights on as I left, Daddy's mouth slack and his nose letting fly a meek whistling, then before the door met the jamb Daddy put up his head and called out I could just crush you to death with love, sweetness.

I walked to the bus stop on the corner, thinking about the scuffs on his shoes and how there was still nothing on his walls and how if you're lonely and drunken I guess it makes sense that you'd be finding meanings everywhere your eyes fell and believing with your whole body in some hillbilly song about the greener side of a hill. But see then when the bus come I seen what Daddy meant about things at night looking different, to look at it the bus some kind of miracle box of light trundling toward me with an offering of strangers and a lungful of air conditioning and a bell I could ring any time I wanted to, to make it stop, but I guess that's not how no tough bitch would talk.

TUESDAY

I came home to my sister pounding on the sliding glass doors. Technically she didn't live there anymore. Technically my dad had thrown her out the night before when she came home at midnight with eyes hard and fogged as marbles and the bitter smell of pot clouding out from her.

I felt bad for her. Her fists up above her head, pounding away. Her spiky black hair. Her shirt bunched up and her belly showing, Such lovely olive skin, our mom used to say, such lovely olive skin threaded with stretch marks and fat now, rippling and rippling like her belly button was the coin dropped in the water. I felt bad for her.

Let. Me. *In*. Behind her the sky was so blue it could've stained your finger. I turned the TV on.

At the commercials I realized she'd been quiet, and when I looked at her I saw her watching me like I'd been watching the TV. I just need my clothes, she said. I walked over to the door and pushed my forehead against it. Did you see the sky, I asked her. Of course, she said. I let her in.

Cunt, she said. In the kitchen she stuck her head in the freezer and sucked at a bottle of vodka. The cold air billowed white around her. Our mom had paid a man to paint angels in my sister's bedroom. They floated in white air.

Want me to help you, I asked her.

Go fuck yourself, she said. Someone on TV started screaming. Here, she said, and handed me the empty bottle. Fill this up with water and put it back in the freezer.

I let the water run and run. I let it fill the bottle and cascade over my hands and fall down the drain. I imagined time slowing until it was nothing, until it dripped like water.

In the freezer I touched my wet finger to a piece of ice and it stuck and my finger got numb. I can endure pain, I wanted to tell her. Better than you.

Hey, she said, and when I turned she was holding our mom's economy-sized bottle of Tylenol. She was chewing. White powder clung to her lips and shirt. Hey, remember when I pierced your ear and we used ice to numb it? She tipped her head back, poured more pills in. You bled like a motherfucker. She coughed and a pill flew out of her mouth and hit my shoulder. She picked it up and wiped it on my shirt. Popping it back in her mouth, she said, Come outside and sit with me.

We sat on the porch and stared at the yard. Her lips were chalked with Tylenol. Light this, she said, handing me a cigarette. Don't inhale or you'll turn evil. She blew smoke rings. Look, she said, halos. She said, you're really annoying, you know that? Good grades and virginity don't count for shit.

Her words were slurring. She held the cigarette up and missed her mouth.

I'm sending up a flare, she said. She pointed at the sky. You see that? I'm sending up a flare. Here I am. Here I am. Here I am.

Her head drooped, her chin touched her chest. Here I am, she said. You don't even have to look to find me.

Evening was coming on. The sky turned pale and the sun was orange and smeared.

When Dad gets home, she said, make him count to ten before he looks for me. No, she said, make it twenty.

KID

Kid was reading his devotional. Then his father came in. His father dragged a chair behind him and it made an embarrassed, resentful sound across the wood floor. His father set the chair under the ceiling fan. Kid read the sentence, Many are the plans in a man's heart, but it is the LORD's purpose that prevails. He read it over and over. His father swiped at the fan's blades with an old dirty rag. Kid read plans in a man's heart plans in a man's plans mans plan man, but he was really wondering what it would be like to fuck a girl in the guts, like right through the belly button. Kid's father said, It makes me so proud to watch you reading your devotionals like that and Kid nodded, thinking girlguts bloodballs. Kid was pretty sure he was some kind of sicko, but at this point he couldn't help it. He made up for his thoughts by being lazy. Like right then he put down his devotional and went into the kitchen and melted some Velveeta over a row of Oreos instead of going down the road to Jenny Bickson's house to see what her innards would feel like on his man place.

Kid's father put on the television. A whole audience of women was screaming mad and Kid imagined their heads in loaf pans in the oven, slices of their doughy faces with butter and jam. On the couch his father had his hand down the front of his pants but Kid knew he was just feeling it, just letting his hand and his balls remember each other. His father put his hand on Kid's head every once in a while in a pride sort of way and it always smelled sour. It always smelled like balls.

His father put his weight on his right leg, farted. His bra strap was hanging down his arm and Kid adjusted it for him as he walked past. Kid's father had titties, said that's what a lifetime of beer and chips did to a man, said a real man dealt with the situation at hand and didn't let his titties flop around like a whore or a fat toddler.

Kid's father said, Walk to the 7-Eleven and get us some dinner, like burritos or cereal or what have you. Hot dogs. Pretzels? Or like Spaghetti-O's or something. Peanut butter and jelly. Frozen pizza. You have choices. I'll pay you back. Oatmeal. Or Cream a Wheat. Whatever. You have choices.

Many are the plans. Kid thought, Many are the plans, yo. Many are the pussies fuckbed lipslits pleasure parade cookie kissnuts. He had seventy-three dollars in the toe of his house slipper. He was thinking Krispy Kremes strawberry milk and pretzel Combos for dinner. Purpose that prevails.

The neighbor had his sprinklers going and the lawn looked like it had been sprinkled with bits of glass. Kid had a stiffy (fuckbed lipslits) and it donged up and down in his pants like a punching clown. He presented it to the late afternoon like Welcome, here is my crotch area, here is what you are seeing, golldang right it's a chub, I am fifteen years old after all. His neighbor was watching a game show, the word Prizes! flashed onscreen. Kid had once watched the neighbor's wife undress, had seen the rolls that bunched at her abdomen when she bent to work off her socks, had lost interest when she started picking at her teeth.

At the 7-Eleven Kid went to the magazine rack and looked at the brides. Some brides had shorter hairstyles and Kid averted his eyes, thinking Nope, that ain't it. Thinking carpets match the drapes? Thinking slut bouquets.

Kid noticed Jenny Bickson in the candy aisle. Just standing around, fingers on the Bubble Tape. Kid thought how Bubble Tape looked like intestines all wound up. Said Hey Jenny, said Grape? Huh-uh, Jenny said, sour cherry. Kid thought Sour cherry, that is right, thought Fingers fingering prevails.

A man came in with red slick hands and yelled for the cashier to call 911, his wife was giving birth in the parking lot. The cashier said, That you at pump two because if so you'll need to move it and the man grabbed fistfuls of his own hair and screamed with his teeth clenched. Kid thought Vagina vagina vagina like it was hanging in red neon in front of his face. Jenny said Someone should boil some water and get some towels. She was standing like she could pee any minute and then she did pee, Kid heard it puddling around her sandals.

154

Kid said Just because they do that on the TV don't mean that's how it's done. The man was still screaming, still holding his hair. The cashier was saying Sir, sir, sir, the phone cradled at her shoulder, Kid thinking If it's a girl a vagina will come out of a vagina, thinking VAGINA. Thinking everything in the world was so sexy, so full of fluid and wet and come coming comer, thinking I could bottle up Jenny's pee and then stick my dick into the bottle and slosh it around, thinking about that sloshing, his junk still donging as he walked past the cashier, past the man, into the parking lot and up to pump number two, where a woman in the backseat of a station wagon was screaming into the face of the baby coming out of her. A crowd was gathering, one boy in an oversized basketball jersey agape, his finger in his ear, digging, the sky was getting that ugly pink it got right before the sun set. Kid thinking Vagina VAGINA menstrual pussy fucky times.

The lady screamed and Kid leaned in and put his hand on the baby's head, pushed, tried to work it back into the hole, thinking Go time, thinking baby blood pudding cup, the lady screaming louder, the lady scratching his cheeks. One of her press-ons came loose and stuck in a cheek gash, Kid thinking Kinky hillbilly porn DNA blend. Thinking Prevails. Kid stuck his fingers inside the lady and grabbed the baby under its arms and pulled, the lady bearing down till her insides turned solid, and the baby coming out so slippery Kid lost his grip and dropped it in the seat. The crowd clapped, someone shouted Yeehoo!, the lady looked up at Kid like she'd puke if she wasn't so empty inside.

Kid went back into the 7-Eleven and bought dinner, plus some Bubble Tape for Jenny. The man was on the phone shrieking Hurry, hurry. There was a glob of the lady's blood on the Bubble Tape container so Jenny wouldn't take it, Kid thinking pee sandals sloe-eyed cobweb crotch.

The sky was a denim color when Kid got home. He heated up the Krispy Kremes in the microwave, his father watching the same game show the neighbor had been, the host mocking a contestant's deep Southern accent, plucking an air banjo. His father laughed, Combos bits flying out his mouth, Kid thinking I put my hands inside a pregnant lady's giner, I'm a golldang hero.

LET

Let's take a ride. I'm your family. Meet me in the basement. Meet me by the Corvette. See that moon? It's a disc of aspirin. See that moon? It's a dollop of jizz. I'm your family. I wear the pants. I find you adorable. Get on the back. Ride the handlebars. Run alongside. Wear this bridle. Kiss a man goodnight. Kiss a man on the lips. You taste like blood. I've tasted blood. You had your blood yet? Touch yourself. I don't have any ideas. Touch your shoulder. Touch my shoulder. Touch yourself. Put my hands on you. Meet me by the tree stump. Take the trail. Leave a trail. Cook me something. Make me a pie. Butter a cracker. Put it in a mouth. Put something in something. You ever been fed? See that moon? It's a pail of milk. See that moon? It's an eye rolled back. You smell like the ocean down there. Let me crouch real close. Let me breathe. Meet me in the pantry. Make us a bowl of something. I'll knock. You'll welcome. Meet me at the movies. I want to see you in the dark. I want to watch your face. Are those elastic? Prove it. I'm your family. Hide. I'll find you. I got the keys. See that moon? It's a white throat. It's a fresh egg. I want to kiss you. I want to put my mouth on you. Make a man feel like a man. Don't talk. Hush up. Cry quiet. Wish on a star. That moon's a lightbulb. Flip the switch. Come to my bedroom. Hang on my wall. I'm your family. Look at the moon. It's a toilet bowl. Hold out your hand. Shake. Put your hands on me. Put your hands inside my coat. I'll hold on. Set. Rise. Lick something. Write down what I'll do. Mail it to me. Lick a stamp. I find you very alluring. Put on a skirt. Act a lady. Point your toe. Fall to your knees. Make your lips the shape of lips. Touch it all up. Press. Leave me something. Wear the mirror. Lean in. Keep quiet. Run the tap. Wash your dirty. Wash that dirty dirty hand. Is that your dress on the line? Show me a stain. Put in that tape. Push play. Let it go. Meet me at the lake. Swim under. Hook a fish, silver for your mirror. I'm your family. I want to wring you out. Drink you from a glass. See that moon? It's a drop of paint. See that moon? It falls up. Take me to the woods. Dig us a spot. Make it round. Climb down. Fall in. Use your fingers. Write my name. Give me a name. Call for me. Say it. Look at that moon, it's a baby's tooth. See that moon? Ladle something in. Fill it up. Cover your eyes. Don't go to sleep. Pull me in. Tell me what to do. Tell me what to do. Tell me what to do.

U S

We dream about throwing baby in the well. We remember our daddy talking stuff about baby holding breath under water, as natural as suckling a breast, something baby just know from birth we'd throw baby underhanded like a softball and it'd land in a dark hole and if there was water baby would hold its breath and if there wasn't.

We go to school with the rest of them. Follow the road, every time it leads us there. Nothing beyond worth mentioning. It's a new school with a black parking lot and a football field and a cafeteria full of windows. On Fridays the lights from the football games and the beat of the drums remind us where we aren't. We dream of the baby in a deep hole, we look under the bed for the baby, the baby is crying and our breasts are wet and the roar of the crowd pulls us into those lights, we wish the lights burn our eyes even though they glow, they only glow, they don't even reach past the middle of the yard, we play the game where we write letters in our hands and spell words, practice talking to each other so we don't make a sound, our favorite letter is B, we spell word after word with it, sometimes the word is blood, sometimes it is baby.

One Monday we are found in the bathroom at school, we are taken to the nurse who asks if we have been familiar with blood, who fingers the tough spots on our clothes and says Has your mother spoken to you about your curse. We hold her hand and write into her palm, blood under our fingernails, we smear red letters, her hand a collection of baby, she calls Daddy. We watch baby gathered into a tissue, we watch baby thrown into the wastebasket, we sit on a bench our thighs sticky the air metallic our hands palm to palm telling a story reaching the end starting over the air warm, alive, how life smells so much like death.

Our daddy picks us up and we are taken for a blessing. We watch the wind in the trees above us, we are on our back, we watch the leaves coming together to form shapes in the sky, we watch the leaves forming other shapes, we are being put together and ripped apart and put together in different shapes like the wind does to the leaves, a man says dominoes, a man says Jezebel, a man says Amen, a man says God almighty, we go home and make dinner, knifing out the eyes in the potatoes, shaping the meatloaf with our hands, Don't wash them, Daddy said, plenty of iron in womanblood, he falls asleep and we make shapes over his face in the blue light of the television: a bird, an alligator, a fist knocking over and over on the pocket of his shirt. Baby, we whisper, baby, are you in there?

Finally we find a boy. He is pale. We see the blue veins behind his ears, one threading from his right eye to his cheek, he shows us a dagger wrapped in a dustcloth at the bottom of his schoolbag, we take him home with us, we lay beside him on Daddy's bed. He says I been watching you, I have named you. We pull up his shirt, we write letters over his heart, he says I know that one, that one's easy but it ain't your name. We say come with us, bring something to show, he brings the dagger. We pull our box out from under the bed, we open it and pull the newspaper away, we show him what we've collected, a few teeth, a purple rock, a used condom, a burned Bible, Daddy's naked circus people cards. We save it for last, pulling it out and laying it in front of our boy, pulling the lace away until we see its gray form, its tiny penis, we see how its mouth has shriveled since we last saw our baby, we see more of its eyes now, we knock on its chest, we show the boy how baby has become a stone. See how black baby's tongue is, we tell our boy. See how thirsty. We hold baby up and feed him, when we lift him we remember how like life death smells, we pick maggots from his legs and pump our breasts.

Our boy is sick down his shirt, another smell, he pushes the dagger in the air around us, he runs the blade down our arm, forcing it in at our elbow. He runs from us, we go to the window and watch him run through the yard, down the road toward school, toward nothing beyond, he disappears. Baby is finished eating, we follow our blood back to our bedroom, we pull out the dagger and give it to baby to hold, baby is covered in blood, is alive, we hear Daddy's truck in the driveway, we cover baby's mouth and nose with our hand. Hold your breath, baby, we say. We will gather maggots in a jar for Daddy. We will go fishing. We will catch baby, reel him in. We will kiss the gash in his cheek. We will throw him back.

FIFTEEN

Tina's mama got us some Boone's. Turtle was on his back in the bathtub upchucking in his sleep. Gin still thought he was cute even as he burbled like a gut fountain. We left her to tend to him. Later on Gin'd be porking Freeman and then Freeman's little brother. We dared Katie to eat what was left in the ashtray and she did. In the corners of Tina's mama's apartment there were little piles of things. Tiny shrines to catshit and dryer lint and wrappers for condoms candy beer-bottles toilet paper lipstick-tubes and various electronics. Tina's mama was a space clearer, is how you could put it. Joey pushed Katie down into the catshit corner and got emphatic in air-grinding over her. Katie had black smudges at the corners of her mouth from the ashtray and it was clear she was working hard to swallow something back. Joey's eyes were closed. Later we realized he was humming that one Journey song. Freeman's little brother was on his back bragging how he could see each individual fan blade in Tina's mama's ceiling fan. His eyes went round and round. Ingalls woke up laugh-crying from what had been an hours-long nap. After he caught his breath he screamed EAT AT THE Y, SUCK IT LIKE A STRAW and then tucked himself back into the couch. It was clear he was a sleep-farter but no one wanted to talk about that just yet. Gin killed the bottle of strawberry-flavored and wondered aloud could kissing Ingalls make the zits near his mouth pop. Freeman's little brother's hand crept up her ankle and she quieted down. Someone noticed the time. So many hours left to fill. With renewed dedication we paired off to make out, which is a real good time-killer. Katie was asleep with her mouth open but Joey got in there and slurped away. Later we'd call Joey Slurpee and he'd punch a wall over it, not least because it was Katie who he'd been kissing, Katie who ate a ashtray and had a uniboob and a mouth with twice the teeth everybody else had, all coated with a even sheen of butter. Tina's mama came out in her undies and a tank top and stood in her flip-flops among us. She pushed at Ingalls' shoulder till he woke up and walked him into her bedroom, holding his arm like a blind man. All the mamas loved Ingalls. He was nearly eighteen so it was alright. Tina's little sister started crying from her crib and Gin stopped making out with Freeman to make a sympathetic sound before Freeman's little brother rolled her over his way. Tina made up a bottle of juice and went in and the baby stopped crying. Suddenly we were tired, guppy-mouthing each other. The room smelled like breath. We heard murmurs from Tina's mama's

bedroom and someone kicked up the fan a notch to drown out the sound. Above it all we could hear the highway just outside Tina's apartment complex, which sounded like what we imagined the ocean to sound like. Joey put his head in Katie's lap. Katie's head lolled until it nestled in the catshit corner. Gin spooned Freeman's brother. Freeman palmed his balls. Turtle hicced once from the bathroom. Tina settled on the carpeting under the baby's crib. In the morning our mamas would pick us up while Tina's mama flipped pancakes to mask the scent of barf and smoke. Our mamas'd drag us to the grocery store, ask what we wanted: Cream of? Instant? 2-minute? Chicken? Meatloaf. Are we out of? Do you need? Ketchup. Mayonnaise.

Lightbulbs? Tampons? Kibble? Your father. Your brother. Go and get. Orange? Cherry? Lime. Are you listening? Do you hear me? Look at me. But all that was later. Ingalls came out of Tina's mama's room in a long T-shirt and rummaged till he found some Twinkies, and then he went back in. The fan whirred and chilled the room. Our mouths tasted like other mouths. We longed for water. The highway inhaled, exhaled. Later we'd tell about how bored we were and what a redneck Tina's mama was. We wouldn't mention how glamorous it felt to say we were bored, and how in the dark we got chill bumps up and down our arms at the idea that this was life, and life smelled like peach carpet spray and cinnamon chewing gum and cheap-flavored wine, all backwashed up.

SEX ARMAGEDDON

To keep warm we play sex armageddon. It used to be called analocalypse. Sex armageddon sounds more serious and less specific.

Anything goes in sex armageddon. Jordan once snorted a Frito and coughed it out onto my breasts, then clapped them together until the Frito was in bits.

We've been living in Jordan's car for about six weeks now, parked on an overlook. In the mornings Jordan meanders down the mountain to wash dishes in the kitchen of a bowling alley. I straighten up the car, read, nap, wash myself with the moist towlettes Jordan brings home. My mother told me I'd amount to nothing if I kept following Jordan around, and she was right. But amounting to nothing is also a job, it takes work, if you let slack a little you can find yourself thinking fondly of the orange walls at the high school you dropped out of, or of the crispy onions your mother sprinkled over your pizza, or of the ceiling you'd look into while you dreamed of being an actress or something.

In the evening Jordan comes back with dinner. Sometimes it's something hot from the kitchen, whatever he can get, a large fries, some jalapeno poppers. Sometimes it's whatever he got from the vending machine. Oreos. Mixed nuts. Fritos.

Tonight it's garlic mashed potatoes and peanut M&M's. Jordan mixes his together, tells me to do the same. This really fat woman fell as she was pitching her ball, he says. Her dress flew up and she had a big old wedge. A triangle of blue M&M shell clings to his lip. It was hilarious, he says.

After dinner Jordan pushes the remnants of our meal to the floorboards, looks at me seriously, and says Okay. His sex armageddon cue.

As always, Jordan plays Satan and commands me, playing God, to bow down to him. I never do, and the battle commences. Jordan's only weapon is his penis, or his demon staff, but I get to use whatever I can find. He pins me, my back against the door handle, and pulls my pants down. I could fight him off, but I never fight him off. In he goes, the Beast, the Fallen, pumping a few good ones and shouting Sur. Ren. Der.

Never, I say. As God, I don't raise my voice. Instead I stick a Bic pen I find in the glove compartment up his ass and cup his balls with my hand, immobilizing him. For a moment he looks like he will swallow his tongue, or come too early. I take the opportunity to pull my legs from under him, push him back, and sit on his face. I command thee to submit, I tell him. I grind his face a little so he can't answer just yet.

Usually Jordan will pull my hair until my face is inches from his demon staff, then command me to suck. I bend a little, so my hair is within his reach, but the second I realize he isn't reaching for my hair, he comes, his body shuddering, his hands hovering near his penis as if to help an old man who might just fall.

I dismount, pulling my pants back on, and he uses the napkins from dinner to clean up. Hoo, he says. Hooee. Then he says, You want me to finish you off or something?

My pants are already back on, I tell him, and he relaxes. The bit of M&M is gone from his lip and I wonder if it's somewhere in my pubic hair. Come here, he says, patting his chest. The napkin is still stuck to his skin and it flutters gently, like paper wings. I put my head on his shoulder and Jordan says We got to keep warm. He rubs my arm a little, then falls asleep, his nose whistling softly, a sweet garlicky smell blowing out of his open mouth.

My mother had given me the talk early. Seven years old. She said The man enters you and fills your emptiness. The man fills you up good and you should enjoy it when it happens.

I come out from under Jordan's arm. Gooseflesh runs across his skin so I put his jacket over him. He doesn't wake up when I open the car door or when I close it behind me.

It's early enough in the fall that it's still light enough out, and I begin walking down the mountain, my bare feet noiseless in the road. I smell sex on myself, salty, bleachlike, moist. I travel in a bubble of sex, sticky skin, used up. The few times Jordan and I have driven up or down the mountain I swear I've seen water, a lake or something, and I plan on using the last of the light to dip in, to make myself smell like anything else—mud, water, or nothing at all.

Jordan says only God can fill an emptiness. First God makes the emptiness, then he fills it.

I hear water moving somewhere close, and then a rustling in the trees. An animal walks out, some kind of big cat, and when it turns its face to me its eyes flash gold. We watch each other for a few seconds, and then I take my cue. Slowly, pushing through the trees, I make my way toward the water, undressing as I go. I don't turn to see if the cat is following. Suddenly I think of the fat woman whose dress flew up at the bowling alley, and I have to fight back tears. I leave my underwear hanging from a sapling. I step into the water, willing the cat to follow, letting the water rush into my ears and over my head, knowing I will let the beast win this time.

I stay under until I can't anymore. Water rushes out of my ears, the cat is gone, the sky is a blue bowl with black edges. I pretend this is a baptism and dunk myself under again. When I come up I see that the black edges are closing in. I make my way out of the water, get myself dressed, and head back to the road, back to Jordan. I'll wake him up, order him to sit on the gear shift. I'm a walking emptiness, a vast nothing, but if I run I can beat the darkness.

WE WAS

There we were in the car with the outsides bleeding by us out the window. Our daddy every once in a while shook his head like he was trying to shake a fly from his ear. His wife wrapped some twine around her pointer finger until it was purple, turned around to smile big into the backseat, Everything's okay children, everything's just fine.

We saw a black bear lumbering along through the trees and Giddy said it was looking for a pot of honey or a stray dog. We passed some red licorice. Carnation had pink foam at the corners of her mouth from all the cramming.

The setting sun made a bruise of the evening sky. Carnation said the sun looked like a dollop of fancy mustard at the horizon.

It seemed like days ago that we'd pulled over and our daddy had yanked Davey out and left him on the highway by a mile marker. They's some jelly beans and limeade in this bag, our daddy said, and dropped a paper sack at Davey's feet. Davey's chin trembled so bad his teeth were chattering and our daddy said Aw suck it up, we'll be seein you. Davey stood in his spot and watched us drive on and in our dust he looked like a spirit. It was mile marker 77.

Daddy's wife asked to pull over so she could empty her jar. We watched her squat over a dead bush a few yards away from the car and pee on into it. Our daddy flicked his head again, whispered, It was his time, you pack of dummies. He was fixin to overpower me. Daddy's wife let down her dress and started walking back. Do you know, our daddy hissed, that Davey would have carved the faces from your bodies and snacked on your flesh like it was a hog's ear?

Carnation told our daddy to unlock the door for his wife. When she got back in she turned around to smile big at us and it was clear by her smell that she'd watered down her leg a little. Our daddy put the car back on the road and peeled his tires.

And then the sky was black as a dog's eye but for where the moon flickered through the trees. Our daddy started humming one of his songs. His wife stumbled along with him, her voice like a choked bird but it was clear she didn't know the tune.

After a while our headlights were sweeping over Grandmother's motel. She came out with an arm over her eyes and our daddy said Goddamn and switched off the lights. She knocked on our window and said, What a snoutful of brass buttons. Her teeth looked like they were hacked from planks and she jangled a ring of keys at us like a witch's charms. You ain't nothing but a pile of wet stars in a bathtub drain. Our daddy said, That's just her idjit way and we got out of the car.

Grandmother dropped the keys and sidewindered away into the darkness. We watched our daddy have his way with his wife in the first room where a key fit, her smiling big and saying, Everything's so wonderful, children, and our daddy working her into the headboard like he was nailing up a granite cross.

We took a bath and watched out the bathroom window. Sure enough Davey's ghost came fluttering in flimsy as a leaf husk and settled on the toilet. We could see right through to the ruby jewel pump in his chest. You want me to I can gather up that navy winking sky and make us a diamondsparkled sail of it, Davey said, and his voice was the same but unnatural, like some busted chorus of bells clattered out his throat along with everything else. We could visit all them quilt patches on the map, but before we could answer Daddy's wife came and sat down to do her business and Davey's ghost burst up like an exploded feather pillow, his parts settling unnoticed on Daddy's wife like how dust is gold in a stream of sunlight but regular and dirty in the no-light. Giddy splashed up some water in disgust and Daddy's wife clapped her hands while the Davey motes shivered off her and fell into the toilet and swirled down to the underworld. God strike you lonely then dead, Carnation whispered and Daddy's wife giggled and pulled up her undies and left us.

Davey's faint jangling still hung in the air and one by one we climbed from the window and jumped. Giddy twisted up her ankle and began to crawl. Grandmother was in the office looking like a drugged specimen in a yellow lightbox, her feet up on the desk and her skirt open and a glint of drool working its way down her neck, and we continued on past her and past the motel itself and into the dark thatchery behind.

It was the moon brought us there. Daddy told us our mother's dumb forlorn soul wafted up to that white eye and got tangled up in its eyelashes, and there the moon was staring wildly from the treetops. Carnation said we was lost and we should pray and sure enough Grandmother's motel had disappeared into a dark nothing behind us, and we knelt in the dirt and held hands and whispered bright nothing prayers and begged for an angel's shovel to dig Davey up from the sewage so he could show us his candied heart once more. We prayed the moon would unstopper long enough to suck us through to the other side so we could see how dull the stars were at their backsides. Far off our daddy began calling for us, and we pretended it was a wolf's howling, or a car rushing down a highway, or that loud emptiness you hear when there's nothing to hear and pretty soon you start believing there never ever was.

LOOFAH

193

He woke up after having a dream of falling. Just before he fell this guy from his college trigonometry class walked toward him shirtless. Then he fell.

He opened his eyes and watched his girlfriend jump around the room on one foot. Charley horse, she yelled accusingly. Her big toe was stuck in the up position. He had a throbbing hard-on and figured it was just as painful.

His throat was dry so he got up and went into the bathroom. He popped a zit in the crease between his nose and cheek and slurped at the water coming out of the faucet. His girlfriend limped in and stood behind him until he met her eyes in the mirror. You could've helped, she said.

What could I have done? he asked her. He answered himself: Nothing. His girlfriend sighed, sat on the toilet with her shirt bunched between her legs. This had always been his dirtiest fantasy, ever since he was a child: a girl's exposed thighs and the delicate sounds of her pee stream hitting the water.

His girlfriend was in a punishing mood. Get out, she said. He leaned over and kissed her forehead, maneuvered his hard-on under the waistband of his boxer shorts.

He found a soft orange in the kitchen with very thin skin. Its insides were blood-colored and dry. He put it back in the fridge and stacked its peels in the middle of the stove.

It was raining outside. He could see a faint reflection of himself in the window. The guy in his dream was shirtless. His girlfriend had beautiful ice-cream-scoop breasts. The guy in the dream was shirtless. His girlfriend had pillowy dicksucking lips. The guy in the dream was shirtless. His girlfriend often played with his balls when she was bored. The guy in the dream was shirtless. His girlfriend got drunk almost every night and breathed Let's get nasty into his ear to the point where the smell of margarita mix got him hard. The guy in the dream was shirtless. His girlfriend let him tie her up once. The guy in the dream was shirtless. His girlfriend the guy in the dream was shirtless.

It's raining, his girlfriend said behind him. She opened the fridge and he stood behind her and tried to finger her. It made him think of the dry bloodcolored orange and he gave it up.

Jake. The guy in his trig class's name was Jake. They'd gone out once, to a frat party, and had ended up making out with two girls who'd been standing by the keg all night. He'd done too many shots of tequila and at the end of it all he'd pushed Jake up against a dumpster on campus somewhere and sucked at his neck. He remembered Jake grabbing his ass and biting his ear, and it turned him on until Jake punched him in the solar plexus and he realized he was getting his ass kicked. He threw up on Jake's shoes and fell asleep on someone's discarded bag of McDonald's. He stopped going to trig and flunked out and had to take an extra semester.

Bagels? his girlfriend asked. Butter? Cream cheese? He'd met his girlfriend at a bar and they'd ended up dry humping against a jukebox playing "Freebird," had been together ever since. I'm not hungry, he said. It thundered loudly and he yelled over it, I gotta take a dump.

In the bathroom he stared at himself in the mirror. He imagined that his body was an elaborate empty coffin. Here lies Nothing. Here lies No One. He could smell the bagel burning in the toaster, heard his girlfriend hiss *Shit*. He masturbated with her mint green loofah and appletini body wash, crouching over the toilet so that when he came there'd be nothing to clean up, no trace of anything ever happening.

MARIE NOE
Talks to You about Her Kids

Always thought babies were dumb. Always did. Bald globey heads and gums dripping spit. Nothing behind the eyes but want. It made me belly-sick to see how they'd reach up for me, needing me to feed 'em and change 'em and hold 'em and hell sometimes just look at 'em. Babies want to be seen more than anything else on this earth. If they aren't bein looked at they don't exist.

Richard farted on his father within the first minute he was born. The whole room heard it, that loud angry gas, Richard announcing hisself in the ugliest of ways, then getting scared I guess and bursting into a cat's wail, the doctor laughing, laughing, saying Well I guess there's no doubt about air in those lungs. Art bent to kiss me and I could smell the baby, could smell the fart, and I turned my face so I could gag into the pillow. At one month Richard died. I told the doctor how I believed a fart got trapped and went back up the other way and into his heart where it all exploded. I cried but I don't remember feeling the need.

Elizabeth was a sloppy eater. She slurped at the breast. And me and Art called her Grabbin Hands because any time she got anywhere near my chest she'd be tryin to latch, even if I had on a sweater, she'd be suckin away, coughin up threads and cat hairs. It disgusted me, how desperate she'd get to feed, but Art thought it was cute. Elizabeth died at five months. She was much stronger than Richard, I remember, but maybe she choked on a lint ball she thought was a nipple. Nobody's fault.

I guess I should confess how I was always kinda scared of babies due to how selfish they were. That might help you to understand my thinkings. Babies would kill you to live.

Jacqueline screamed with her eyes wide open, looking straight at me. Like this. And when she slept she'd be chanting in a demon's language. I planned on calling her Jackie, but she didn't make it past ten days old.

Art says after Jacqueline we had a boy we named Arthur Jr., that he only lived five days. I suppose he's right.

Constance was a moron. She never even opened her eyes, though Art swears she had one blue one and one brown one. By the time she was born I'd had a headache for two years straight, and the fact that she never made a sound, didn't look at me, slept through the night, that weighed more on me than any kinda screaming she coulda done. Like her quiet was creating a noise louder than all the other babies combined. It split my ears. I'd pinch her till she'd cry to make up for it, and I guess that's wrong. She was dead after 24 days. Art went downtown one night and got the word Constance tattooed on his upper arm and when he came home I told him what a idiot he was.

I knew Letitia was dead inside me for days before she was born, but I let her stay inside. That was one of the happiest times in my life, me and the baby sharing a death. When I think back on that time it's all white, like I was livin in a white room with white curtains and the beach just the other side of the window. After the stillbirth I acted sad for Art's sake. I pulled his head down over my heart and let him cry, and he promised to never reach for me in bed again, but I broke him down after a couple of years. I always liked being pregnant, it's a woman's duty.

The doctor asked me once, was there something about the dead children I wanted to confide. But I had disliked him ever since he ate a sandwich during one of my appointments, right there in the examining room, so I told him if I had anything to confide the only one who'd know was Art.

When I found out I was pregnant again, the doctor had me and Art come in for parenting classes, a bunch of nurses showing us how to hold the baby, how to burp the baby, how to make sure the baby isn't being suffocated by something in its crib, how to keep the baby alive. Art was so serious, takin notes and askin questions. He was afraid of losin another child, but I don't get afraid like that. Fear is for people who don't take charge.

Mary Lee looked like my mother, and she cried all the time like my mother did too. I rubbed rum on my nipples at feeding time to calm her down because rum used to also settle my mother. Mary Lee died at nearly seven months. Then *Life* magazine did a story on Art's and my bad luck at having kids, and everywhere we'd go people recognized us. Our favorite restaurant even gave us free dinners for a year. I had the steak every time we went, rare.

Theresa never even left the hospital. I don't recall what she looked like. Art says she had a full head of hair, but I don't remember seeing any baby like that come out of me. Anyway. She was alive for less time than it took for me to push her out.

The doctor got on me to stop procreating, to refuse Art in bed, but the doctor had it backwards. I wanted it more than the doctor knew, so bad it scared Art. One night he asked Is this normal? But if it wasn't I didn't care.

They kept Catherine at the hospital for a number of weeks, to make sure she wasn't going to pass like the others I guess. Me and Art visited her once during that time but the drive was such a chore. When we picked her up the doctor held his hand over her forehead like a blessing and told me to call day or night. When I was a child my mother held my hand to the hot stove to teach me not to touch it ever again, and Catherine was such a willful child that I had to teach her the same lesson when she was just a year. I guess I held it there for too long because she lost some skin, and then she quit breathing so me and Art drove her to the hospital and left her there a few days. My headaches were back for the first time since my time with Letitia, and Catherine talked so much, all of it gibberish, that I felt anger towards her, my own child. She was dead a few months after her first birthday, choked on one of Art's dry cleaning bags, or it was crib death again, I don't know.

The last child was Arthur Jr. Guess Art really wanted a Jr. I got to calling him Arty. I lost my uterus because of Arty. He was a fat baby, his eyes like dull buttons about to pop, and maybe that's why my uterus ruptured, and maybe that's why his heart failed him at six months, because it was already clogged with fat, useless. He made noises when he fed, moans of satisfaction, and even now I shudder to think about that.

I had ten children with Art, and ten children died. That's nobody's fault. Dead is dead. It was years ago. We have a rose garden. We have cats. Our staircase has seventeen steps. I have my hair washed and set every Tuesday. Those babies are in a graveyard Art and I drive by on the way to the grocery store. Tonight we'll have meatloaf and corn on the cob. Richard Elizabeth Jacqueline. Arthur Jr. Constance Letitia. Mary Lee Theresa Catherine Arthur Jr. Two Arthur Jrs. See I think Art agrees with me. They weren't any of em different from the others.

W E

We were walking the backyard. Pacing it out. One, we said. Two. And on and on. It's true, we told our brothers, this backyard's a grave. In the window our mother's face fell. She waved a hand at the ax. We took turns and soon the tree slumped against the fence. Our brothers carried it on their backs and offered its heart to our mother. We're hungry, they said. We're starved. Our mother's eyes didn't meet ours and our brothers put the tree back on its stump. We watched it fall again. Again, our brothers said, and we said, One. Two. Our brothers axed a hole in the ground and jumped in. We pushed the dirt over them. The neighbor's swingset creaked and moaned next door and we heard a child's voice say Never ever. We planted the ax in the mound over our brothers. The ax blade was bloody with dirt. We tried to see ourselves in it. In the window our mother forked stars into a piecrust, said See, this is also a grave.

ACKNOWLEDGMENTS

Special thanks to Sam Axelrod, Megan Baker, Allison Burque, Landry Miller, Audrey Niffenegger, and Brandon Will.

Further thanks to the editors of the following journals in which some of the stories in *Daddy's* appeared, including:

"The Fence" appeared in *Nerve*.

"Unpreparing" appeared in *Hobart*.

"Scales" appeared in *Night Train*.

"Tuesday" appeared in *Smokelong Quarterly*.

"It All Go By" appeared in *Thieves Jargon*.

"We" appeared in *elimae*.

"Peggy's Brother" appeared in *Knee-Jerk*.

"Finding There" appeared in *Cricket Online Review*.

"We Was" appeared in *Somnambulist Quarterly*.

"Loofah" appeared in *Fiction at Work*.

"Food Luck" appeared in *ACM*.

"Marie Noe Talks to You about Her Kids" appeared in *Proximity* and was performed at the Encyclopedia Show on serial killers.

"That Baby" appeared in *Everyday Genius*. Special thanks to guest editor and bloodeater Blake Butler.

"My Brother" appeared as a featherproof mini-book, which maybe started this whole book thing. Billowing thanks and love to Zach Dodson and Jonathan Messinger.

Lindsay Hunter lives in Chicago, where she runs the flash fiction reading series, Quickies! Her short fiction has been published widely online. This is her first book.

featherproof
BOOKS

WE PUBLISH STUFF

featherproof books is an indie publisher dedicated to doing whatever we want. We live in Chicago and publish idiosyncratic novels and downloadable mini-books, as well as 333-word stories for the iPhone. Visit featherproof.com, OK?

---

coming **NOVEMBER 2010**

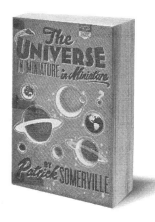

The Universe in Miniature in Miniature by Patrick Somerville

In this genre-busting book from award-winning novelist Patrick Somerville characters, stories, and stray thoughts revolve around the "The Machine of Understanding Other People," the story of a Chicago man who is bequeathed a supernatural helmet that allows him to experience the inner worlds of those around him. Through his lonely lens we peer into the mind of an art student grappling with ennui, ethics and empathy as she comes to terms with her own beliefs in a godless world. We telescope out to the story of idiot extraterrestrials struggling to pilot a complicated spaceship. We follow a retired mercenary as he tries to save his marriage and questions his life abroad. Mind-bending and cracklingly new, Somerville's broadly appealing and uniquely imaginative constructions probe the outer reaches of sympathy, death, and love in a world seen from the inside out.

NOVEMBER 2010, $14.95
978-0-9825808-1-3, eBook: 978-0-9825808-9-9

www.*featherproof*.com

BOOKS

The Awful Possibilities by Christian TeBordo

A girl among kidney thieves masters the art of forgetting. A motivational speaker skins his best friend to impress his wife. A man outlines the rules and regulations for sadistic child-rearing. A teen in Brooklyn, Iowa, deals with the fallout of his brother's rise to hip hop fame. You've heard these people whispering in hallways, mumbling in diners, shouting in the apartment next door. In brilliantly strange set pieces that explode the boundaries of short fiction, Christian TeBordo locates the awe in the awful possibilities we could never have imagined.

The Awful Possibilities by Christian TeBordo ($14.95, 978-0-9771992-9-7, eBook: 978-0-9825808-7-5)

Scorch Atlas by Blake Butler

A novel of 14 interlocking stories set in ruined American locales where birds speak gibberish, the sky rains gravel, and millions starve, disappear or grow coats of mold. In 'The Disappeared,' a father is arrested for missing free throws, leaving his son to search alone for his lost mother. In 'The Ruined Child,' a boy swells to fill his parents' ransacked attic. Rendered in a variety of narrative forms, from a psychedelic fable to a skewed insurance claim questionnaire, Blake Butler's full-length fiction debut paints a gorgeously grotesque version of America, bringing to mind both Kelly Link and William Gass, yet turned with Butler's own eye for the apocalyptic and bizarre.

Scorch Atlas by Blake Butler ($14.95, 978-0-9771992-8-0)